LET THERE BE LIGHT

A Diwali Story

By Siva K. C. Penamakuru

Illustrated by Sara Kuba

TO MY WIFE, KIDS, AND FAMILY. AND TO
EVERYONE, WHO LOVES DEEPAVALI.

Table of Contents

LET THERE BE LIGHT
A Diwali Story

Introduction

In a distant solar system similar to ours, there is a planet like Earth which has various Dvipas aka continents, Samudras aka oceans, Nadhis aka rivers—

Wait—How is that even possible?

It is possible. The universe is full of mysteries. This planet has an atmosphere, topography, and various natural components similar to Earth.

Then why do scientists not know about it?

Not everything is known to science yet. Ok? This planet which mimics Earth also has people living there called pasumans. They are like humans.

If it is not known to science yet, how do you know about it?

I will explain, but first, let me continue. Pasumans are like humans on Earth, just that they look like animals but are not quite animals. A pasuman who resembles a lion, has two legs and two hands like a human but a lion's face and body. And they differ in height, weight, and color too, just like humans—

This is not even possible scientifically.

In addition to pasumans, this Earth-like planet has some normal animals too...

Enough, all this sounds silly and dumb.

Ok, Ok... I tried!... And now that I read it, it does sound silly. I love animals and wanted to write a nice festive story with animal-like characters residing on this mythical planet. So now, take that science hat off, put on the fun hat and go with the flow without interruptions. On this planet, there is this beautiful continent called Vajra Dvipa, which has a large variety of flora and fauna and a hugely diverse population of pasumans. It has a temperate climate in the north, subtropics in the north-central and central regions, and tropical monsoons further down south. In this story, you come across five main characters.

The Pulis: Adhvika (Ah-d-v-ih-k-aa) and Aadi (AA-d-ee). They resemble tigers.

The Gajas: Sumati (Su-mati) and Subbu (Sub-bu), the elephant pasumans.

Jambu (Jam-bu) Ballu, the bear pasuman.
And there are a few more that get introduced as the story progresses.

The story itself is set on Diwali day, showcasing the various traditions of the festival and how these five get together to celebrate it. During the celebrations, they become a part and cause of some not-so-good experiences and how they overcome those while discovering the true essence of the festival, forming the story's crux. Before we begin the story:

• If you are interested to know why Diwali is even celebrated, read Jambu's letter at the end of the book. While he claims to be no guru, his life is full of experiences he gathered from living in different places, meeting pasumans of different cultures, and making many connections during this time. So, he has a lot of wisdom to share.

• There is a detailed glossary at the end of the book. Use it only as a quick reference guide for the meanings and context of different words in this book. Some of them have a much deeper meaning than suggested in this glossary. (Example Brahma-Muhurta, Mantra, Mudra, etc.).

• Some words have been used interchangeably. For example, Diwali vs. Deepavali, Dussehra vs. Dasara, and Diya vs. Deepa.

• The book is written in U.S. English; Therefore, some of the spellings might seem off for U.K./Indian English readers. For example:
    o Colorful (U.S.) – Colourful (U.K./India).
    o Neighborhood (U.S.) – Neighbourhood (U.K./India).

So why wait? Let's get going... Happy Deepavali!

Chapter 1:

Aarambha – The Festival Day Beginning

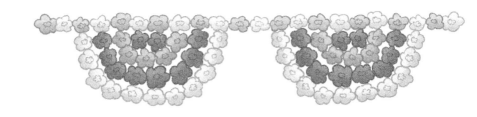

Somewhere in the *Uttara Vajra Dvipa* it was barely dawn, and being an Amavasya almost, in the peaking autumn season, it looked much darker than usual. There was fidgety quietness in the air that seemed to pave into an impending storm. What else to expect? It's Diwali day!!

Trrrrriiiiinnnnnnnggggg...

Adhvika sprung up to a screeching alarm sound. She didn't sleep well that night. Too many things on her mind.

"Wake up!" she yelled anxiously.

"S'it—mornin'—already? I want—sleep," mumbled Aadi dazedly, trying his best to open his eyes as he struggled to reach the alarm to switch it off.

"We haven't even started any decorations yet. There is so much work to do. Let's get going!" Adhvika insisted as her swollen wrinkled-looking eyes testified to the tiredness.

"Ugggh!" said Aadi as he slowly rolled over and dragged himself out of bed groggily.

Diwali in Pulis' house is a serious business. It's very unusual for them that their house let alone be festive ready, looked as if badly shaken from a tremor. Dust all over, clothes everywhere, unwashed utensils. It's a sight best not spoken about. Why, though? You might wonder. Hmm...a long story...

Pulis loved traveling. They at least thought so. Well, they spoke much more about it than they actually did, anyways. Just a few weeks ago, they called the Gajas and invited them over to visit and stay for Diwali. Gajas lived in the *Dakshina Vajra Dvipa*. In the call, Aadi, as usual, went on a tangent about their travel to the beautiful Astagiri mountains and the hiking adventure they undertook on the famous Vikasa trail. A fifteen-mile hike with multiple waterfalls, a pathway through the rolling hills, and beautiful valley viewpoints. The original plan was to reach the other side of the trail and stay the night in

Moorva Town. They started early, before sunrise. But the unexpected inclement weather they ran into had other plans as it slowed down their hike. By dusk, they were about halfway into the hike with seven more miles to go. The weather didn't seem to cooperate. Aadi's over-cautious and diligent packing of a large version of Battu's camping essentials kit came in handy. It had about fifty items ranging from a tent for sleeping to a toy for playing if they got bored. Adhvika's grudge was that all that extra luggage slowed them down considerably. Aadi differed. The ten pictures they took for every five steps had put them in a fix was his argument. Nevertheless, they camped that night in the distant woods near a stream on the trail.

Adhvika had many concerns, though. They were amateur campers after all. *Would there be snakes? How could they survive lest they encountered one?* She feared. *No worries, snakes don't enter tents*, Aadi was sure. *And the tent is zipped anyways*, he reassured. *But what if it cuts through using its fangs?* Adhvika wondered. Aadi waved off, pointing to Battu's snakecapturing bag. *But then, what about bears or tigers?* She continued with her worries. Aadi dismissed the unreasonable fears. They had Battu's repellents, from tigers to bears and even bugs. He didn't pack all of those for no reason. After his buoyant reassurance and comforting, they settled down and slept.

In the middle of the night, Aadi woke up with what he thought he felt was a wiggle. He ignored it and tried to go back to sleep. But he felt the wiggle again, and this time he also heard a hissing sound. He thought it was definitely a snake that was moving below the tent. So he jumped from sleep frantically, woke up Adhvika and tried to look for any movement again. Adhvika irritatedly suggested it was probably the sound from the wind and the wiggle was from a twig he rolled over on. Not convinced, he clutched Battu's snake-capturing bag and watched for himself and Adhvika for the next couple of hours as she snored away to glory. He didn't know when, but he fell asleep eventually as well.

They woke up startled by a grunting noise at the crack of dawn. It was still dark, partly due to the trees that obscured any feeble light. They couldn't exactly see what it was. Aadi sure thought it was a bear that made a ruckus of all the garbage and other belongings they left outside the tent. Adhvika differed. She thought it was just a raccoon. *But do raccoons make such a loud grunting noise? Silly Adhvika!* he sniffed in his mind as he partially unzipped the tent, took the bear repellent, and pressed it with all his might. It didn't work. Then he tried the tiger one, but no luck, followed by hyena, vulture, and fox, all in vain until the slug one went off. Adhvika doubted if that would work on a bear or a raccoon. *A repellant is a repellant. How would animals know which one is what?* Reasoned Aadi as he offloaded half of the bottle ferociously, though most sprayed within the tent. As they coughed and suffocated with the strong repulsive odor, Adhvika just unzipped the tent and went out. The animal, whatever it was, was long gone by then. Adhvika was mad that her sleep got disturbed while Aadi fumed at her ingratitude. In his mind, he made sure they survived a snake and bear adventure right

there that night.

Pulis' immediate family, extended family, friends, and everyone else in the neighborhood knew about this travel survival adventure. This trip was from three years ago after all. So on that Diwali invitation call, Aadi was probably narrating this story for the fifty-third time. Subbu Gaja had heard it many times before, but almost every time, he was curious about how the Pulis just survived on some paneer and meat slices they roasted in the fire that night. *What fun is walking this laddoo trail in the wilderness with no civilization? Even if they did, they should have completed the trail to reach Moorva town or run back to the starting point when the weather went bad so that they could have had a nice, sumptuous meal in a cozy hotel room,* he thought. Sumati Gaja never had any of it. *Why would anyone go all the way to Vikasa trail but not capture any finer details or the larger vivid nature in the background,* she scoffed. All those strange and artificially staged poses of Pulis jumping over a stream, hanging from a branch, smelling a flower, faking a fall on a slope, Yoga Asana on a rock, sitting in the middle of a trail with irrelevant tree branches in the background didn't impress her. When this long-wounded, adventure-narration-bounded invitation call ended, Gajas agreed to travel and celebrate Diwali with the Pulis.

And then, as Diwali approached, Pulis, as in every year, took some time off from work to make elaborate preparations for the festival but just like that an opportunity arose that led them in a different direction. They found a great last-minute deal to travel to Sakaii Dweepam. Travel after three years? They couldn't let go of, that too, to their favorite island for a very attractive price. So they went with it and just returned from that trip late last night, grabbed as many groceries as they could before crashing for the night. And then they are in an unprepared house and expecting Gajas in a few short hours.

Adhvika looked around the house with a deep sigh and said, "Why don't you start cleaning the house? I'll start washing the dishes and then make meal preparation. Don't forget to remove those clothes."

"Don't sweat honey, I'll order some food from outside," said Aadi hoping she would divvy up the cleaning tasks with him.

"Order food? Huh! I plan to make all our favorite dishes. How can we just have outside food on Diwali?" snapped Adhvika. Was it mentioned already? Diwali is no joke for Pulis. And Adhvika took pride in her cooking and hosting.

With no other option, Aadi acknowledged and grabbed the broom and started sweeping the house while she got busy washing the dishes, cutting vegetables and fruits, mixing different kinds of flour, roasting and grinding lentils, and frying various ingredients in ghee. As Pulis got immersed in their respective tasks, their thoughts wandered.

While Sakaii was their dream vacation, rushing it at the last minute before Diwali wasn't right, thought Adhvika. They couldn't even do half the activities. Snorkeling was high on their list, and beloved Aadi took a few steps into the ocean from the beach, put his face inside the water, and declared he saw yellow and gold-colored fish. That sure might have been the sand and reflection from sunlight, thought Adhvika, as she couldn't find a fingerling, let alone a fish, even after she swam into the ocean. The other time she pulled him to the middle of the ocean as part of a snorkeling trip, Aadi, who wore inflatable arm floats and hung onto a noodle, swallowed lots of water and splashed like a hapless fish on the shore. She had to remove his face mask for him to breathe and calm down. And then the second one on the list was hiking. The two-surprise waterfall hikes that Aadi planned and spent an hour packing for were all fifteen minutes long and very underwhelming. So what is the point of this trip? While all is not his fault, she, too, was into it and couldn't let go of a nice travel deal. Lesson learned. *No more rushing into travel without proper planning, as much as they like to do it,* she thought. *Especially not before Diwali, anyway.*

Aadi, on the other hand, was thinking of a relaxing vacation when he found this deal. Lazing on a beach with pina colada was all he dreamt of. But the snorkeling trip, the two 'disappointing as per Adhvika' hikes, the random sightseeing with pictures posing galore, morning beach runs, evening dinner and dance cruise, and the resort complimentary 'fire and water' yoga that reminded him of the one-time gymnastics class he took during his elementary school years, all this packed in such a short duration left him sore and exhausted. *Why did I even spot a travel deal when all she wanted me to look for was Diwali gifts?* he wondered.

"Hmm, bad decision... bad decision," he murmured. At least he should have properly communicated his idea of a vacation to her—

"Terrible decision!" he snorted. Well, on the brighter side, he now has a story to tell—*How we braved water in the middle of the ocean,* he smiled to himself.

As they finished their thoughts, so did the work get completed. And in the next few hours, the house began to look clean. It filled up with overwhelming yet hunger-stirring smells. Adhvika finished frying the last round of pakodas, then they had a quick brunch and settled down to rest.

Chapter 2:

Aagamana – The Arrival

After a while, the doorbell rang...

"The Gajas are here, I think," yelled Adhvika in excitement. Aadi opened the door as Subbu and Sumati stepped in.

"Happy Deepavali!" said Subbu.

"Happy Diwali to you, too!" replied Adhvika.

"Welcome, please come in," said Aadi.

"Here is some pulihora and payasam..." Sumati gushed.

"Ah! pulihora," said Subbu. "We prepared it this morning before heading out to the airport. We added some extra spice to pack a punch."

"But it's me that prepared it. Not *we*...got up at Brahma-Muhurta hour to do this," said Sumati in a soft voice.

"Ah!—of course, it's you, dear." He smiled but immediately changed into a very thoughtful look. "Aadi, are you a peanut or a cashew nut guy?"

"Err—cashews...I guess..."

"I thought so. I am a peanut guy too. They have a unique, strong, and distinguished flavor. Love it! So...we added roasted peanuts to this rice. The peanuts go 'hey, I am going to dominate all the flavorrr...'" said Subbu in a spooky voice and then changing into a dramatic tone "'Hold your laddoo-excitement peanuts! We won't let you have all the fun', say the tamarind pulp, jaggery, and green chilis with their tanginess to counter. And then—suddenly from nowhere—'hello dear, I am here...' says hing with its pungency. And to finish it off, tempering in mustard oil with curry leaves. Ohh, can't wait to eat this." He grinned, smacking his lips while narrating the recipe of pulihora.

Sumati rolled her eyes and was about to give the food she had packed carefully in the boxes to Adhvika.

"Let's have some pakodas," said Adhvika in elation.

"Ah! Sounds delicious," said Subbu satisfyingly.

"You just had lunch in the airport..." whined Sumati with her arms out. "He was bawling like a hungry baby as soon as we got off the flight. We had to grab a supposedly quick bite which turned into a heavy meal as we got five orders of them."

"Oh! You started so early in the morning, probably had to skip breakfast," reasoned Aadi.

"He had kumbhams of pulihora before starting and a snack on the flight too," snapped Sumati, gritting her teeth.

"But how can a lunch end without a garam masala chai made by Adhvika?" smirked Subbu diverting the topic.

Adhvika beamed with pride. "Pakodas and chai are coming your way." And she went inside.

"Ugh!" shrugged Sumati as she put the food boxes she was still holding on the table.

As Subbu continued with his food endeavors, "Hey—no decorations yet? That too in Pulis' house. How can that be?" said Sumati, deviating from the conversation.

"That's a long story..." said Adhvika, handing over the pakodas and some kaju katlis to the Gajas and Aadi.

"Yes, we went on a last-minute trip," responded Aadi.

"Ah! The one on that trail when—what was it—a bear? Crawled underneath you while you were starving?" said Subbu chomping the pakodas.

"It was a snake!" said Aadi.

"A twig!" snapped Adhvika.

"Adhvika thinks twigs move... hmm, it doesn't matter. This is different. We went to Sakaii Dweepam," said Aadi.

"Sakaii? Wow!" exclaimed Sumati.

"The crunchiness of this pakoda...with that contrast from the moistened onion within..." *slllrrrrrrrrrrrrrrrr*... "Aaahh!! The ginger infused garam chai..." blabbered Subbu in a trance as he relished the offerings and wasn't listening to the conversation.

"I don't mean to interrupt. We can talk about the trip leisurely. But I need help setting up the decorations. As you can see, we didn't even begin them," said Adhvika nervously.

"For sure! What's the plan?" asked Sumati in a soothing tone.

"I'll let you handle the rangoli. You are very artsy, Sumati. But for the flowers and the diyas I have some ideas."

"Yes. I have some good muggu and kolam designs in mind with nice flowery patterns!"

"I also ordered a brass diya while I was on vacation. It's very tall and good-looking. That would go in the center of the hallway. It should come in at any moment. We couldn't set up the Diwali decor in time for you to enjoy, but at least if we complete the decorations, it would be good to see Jambu's reaction when he comes in."

"Yes, of course! Let me get started and develop some patterns," said Sumati as she took a paper and pen.

Jambu was a dear friend of Pulis and Gajas. He was a decade and a bit older than them, a teacher by profession but disliked the organized and limited regiment of the schools. He never stayed put with any one school, changed places frequently, and finally decided it was not for him. He was a man of sturdy and studious demeanor in general, but often let his inner child loose when he was with the Pulis and Gajas. That is what he liked the most being with them.

He was invited too, to join them again this year for the festival, to which he gratefully agreed and confirmed he would be there for the evening celebration and dinner.

And then, a loud knock on the door captured everyone's attention.

"That must be the diya I was talking about..." exclaimed Adhvika.

"Jambu!" said Aadi, surprised but happy as he opened the door.

"Happy Diwali. Hope you don't mind me showing up early. My other plans got canceled."

"No, not at all. Please come in..."

"I got some flower garlands," said Jambu, placing them on the table and looking around with widened eyes. "No decorations yet..." That wasn't a question to Pulis. Rather self-astonishment. There was never a Diwali in the past many years that Jambu has been a part of when Pulis' house wasn't all prepped up and ready days in advance like a freshly honed jewel.

"Pakodas?" offered Aadi.

"No, thank you. Done with my morning food. Will have it only in the evening again," said Jambu casually.

"It's Diwali! You need to taste some," insisted Adhvika.

"Hmm... You know what... Let me take one. Can't just say no to festive food," said Jambu.

"Pfff... Morning food done? Only one pakoda now?" snorted Subbu shaking his head at Jambu.

"What's going on? I had to double-check before entering the house. No lights yet? Very unlike you," said Jambu finally.

"Hmm... a long story. I now need all your help with the festive preparation," pleaded Adhvika.

"Sure, tell me what I can do," said Jambu, clasping his hands.

"We are ready when you are Adhvika," assured Sumati.

Aadi nodded in agreement.

"I'll be right behind you..." said Subbu, finishing up the leftover food.

"Alright. Let me go and get all the decor items, and then let's devise a plan," said Adhvika as she went inside. It was almost afternoon...

Chapter 3:

A Quest for that Perfect Diwali!!

Five people working on the festive decor shouldn't take that long. A few hours is a lot of time if they divide the tasks among themselves. Yet, as much as Adhvika wanted the rest to help, she wasn't comfortable. On the one hand, she was too particular about how her decorations should be. From the lights outside the house to the flowers at the entrance, from rangoli to mehendi designs, and from the wall decor to the food she made. It was always her direction and decision. Aadi was a very helpful partner in that. But today—today is different. She doesn't have the luxury of time to coordinate and oversee all this. She has her friends now to help. But then, Jambu is many things, but he doesn't have the delicate touch. Crafty things are not the strongest of his suits, and he was sometimes very clumsy. Sumati, no question on her talent. Rangoli and mehendi designs are her forte, even better than Adhvika. But she is a victim of her own diligence and can get lost in the art of perfection. For instance, during last year's Navratri mehendi session, she took six hours and put 15 patterns within a small square on the left corner of Adhvika's hand. So time stipulation would be the key, albeit without offending her.

Subbu loves to eat but cooks well too—not many realize. He likes to help people and does a good job of helping people on a good day. But that good day which rarely comes, could that be today? It didn't seem so, based on how he was still going on a monologue on the kaju katlis now that he was done with the pakodas. And good old Aadi, who was supposed to be Adhvika's partner here, is distracted. He didn't look to be in the Diwali spirit today and seemed to have a hangover from the trip. Adhvika brought all the decoration items from last year and put them on the floor in the hallway.

"The waves were all over me. I had to keep my face up with a mask full of water while the waves were pulling me down..." said Aadi animatedly, moving his arms as if he was swimming.

Subbu was sitting on the couch, his hands behind his head, eyes closed, and legs stretched onto the ottoman while still ruminating on the last piece of katli.

Was he even listening? wondered Adhvika.

"This guy had some sutli bombs tied up as a ladi and was blasting them on the road. Can you believe the level of noise they made? Is this the real festive spirit? I had a fight," said Jambu strongly.

"A fight, like a real fist fight?" gasped Sumati.

"Fight, as in, I reasoned with words. Albeit angrily. Fun comes with limitations and responsibility. This is obnoxious," said Jambu sternly.

Adhvika was getting worried each minute as she sorted the decor items and tried to plan out everything. *Where is the brass diya I ordered?* She screamed in her mind. The status shows out for delivery since morning. And then she realized there were no clay diyas left either from last year. *This is not happening,* she thought. She had pictures of every single Diwali decor from the past many years. How different and good they were each time. But also, maybe she was overreacting. *Like, really, how bad could it get?* She contemplated. There was still a lot of time left. In the end, that's ok. It is just one Diwali. If the decor doesn't turn out well, she can still have a good time. Isn't that the festival spirit, to have a good time? And the food turned out to be good. *So what's this fuss all about anyway?* She comforted herself philosophically.

But then, it's just not about her. Two of her neighbors have visited so far this day to exchange goodies and wishes. They were surprised that the house was not festive ready yet, *very unusual for Pulis,* they both thought. Adhvika had to explain about the trip, but who was listening? They all went raving about the rangoli setup in Mrs. Bagh's house. Ugh! If there was one thing Adhvika bested Bagh and her petty politics in, it was Diwali!

All these years, Pulis' house was adjudicated unofficially to be the best for Diwali decorations in the entire neighborhood. And Adhvika wouldn't let this year be different either, could she? And somewhere inside, it's not even about what others think. Diwali is too important for her and Aadi. And it's not like this day happens every month. So she avowed "Pulis' Diwali never fails," in a low stern voice.

"Here is the plan," she said loudly, alerting everyone. "Sumati and I would start doing the rangoli. Sumati, if you can do the centerpiece, I'll do it along both the walls in the hallway leading up to the entrance."

Sumati nodded with a thumbs-up.

"The walls must be decorated with these curtain lights and flower garlands. Thank you, Jambu, for the garlands," she acknowledged. "And then the lights have to be set up outside the house too. We also need to get some diyas and fireworks from the market for the night."

Aadi and Subbu decided to set up the outside lights while Jambu offered to do the wall decorations. The plan was set, and everyone got to their work. As time passed, Sumati almost finished putting what she called kolam/muggu outside the main door on the porch. Adhvika was elated, as she almost forgot about deciding to decorate that part of the house. Sumati started with just putting the dots, counting, and correcting them. Once she had the required grid, she started from the top and went in a repeating hand motion connecting dots with lines in such a fashion that they looked like flower petals intertwined. She went on and on until connecting the very last dot. She just had to add color now. It was always a delight to watch Sumati bring these designs to life. *Bravo*

Sumati! She is doing well on time today, thought Adhvika. She too was making good progress with beautiful patterns on the floor and all along the walls. Aadi and Subbu decided to keep things simple and just hang the lights all along the corner of the roof. They didn't have enough hanging clips, so they started taping them instead.

"If there are any lights left after this, we can make a design on the wall there," said Subbu pointing to the exterior wall near the porch.

"Hmm, using the lights? What design do you think?" asked Aadi.

"Ya! Something that signifies and reminds us of Deepavali."

"Bravo, Subbu. Interesting idea. Could it be like a rangoli flower design?"

"Ugh. Nahhhh..." said Subbu in an elongated grunt. "We have enough rangoli in the house. I was thinking of something like a big circle..." he said thoughtfully.

"Circle?"

"Yeah, like a big round."

"How does that remind anyone of Diwali?"

"Laddoo... no laddoos no Diwali."

Aadi gave a grimacing look.

"What? Just a thought," said Subbu as they both returned to work.

Phwee phwee phwee phweeeeeeettttt... phwoo phwoo phwoo phwoo phwoooooootttt...

Jambu whistled as he completed hanging the curtain lights along both the walls in the living room and was now making a banner of sorts using the flower garlands. He hung each garland in a semicircle fashion, tying them to the thread which went horizontally from one end to the other. Each one started at the point where the previous one ended. And these made a series of beautiful U-shaped garlands—Well, that was the idea anyway, and he, in his mind, was doing a phenomenal job, but just that they didn't exactly turn out that way. These semi-circles looked as if they were crunched by a stomach bug, a bit wonky, elongated on one side, uneven and not that appealing. And then the curtain lights didn't look even either. There was a slant to them. And to add some more annoyance to the pudding, the lights went all the way to the end on one side while on the other side, there was a significant gap from the corner to where the lights ended. And these things mattered to Adhvika.

"Jambu..." she whispered with shortened eyes as if they were twitched. "Those need some adjustment. They are not symmetric." Pointing to the garlands as she couldn't let go of these things any longer.

"Really?" said Jambu, taking a step back, adjusting his glasses and peering at the wall decor with his mouth open as if to catch a fish that just jumped out of water. "Ooh. A slight correction needed," he grunted, making it sound very easy while pulling the shortened side of the garland down as if it would self-adjust. When it didn't work, he applied more force.

Thuppp...

The garland and the thread it was tied to, broke on one end, bringing down the entire series and leaving it hanging from the other.

"Hahahaha!! Oh...." he laughed in a cough-howling voice. "No worries, no worries will fix it back." As he wobbled to pick them from the floor.

"No problem, Jambu. I'll be with you as soon as I finish this corner. Okay…" said Adhvika in a long-trying hard to be courteous-voice that sounded like a haunting song or a whistling rocket before bursting into fire. Well, rocket or not, there were fireworks inside her for sure.

Sumati finished her work outside and started on the rangoli inside. After some time, the doorbell rang. Adhvika went to the door eagerly, hoping it was the diya. She felt a cold lump in her stomach as she opened the door.

"Hi, Adhvika dear, Happy Diwali…"

In all these years that Pulis celebrated Diwali in that neighborhood, not once did Mrs. Bagh stop by their house to wish them. But here she was, in full glory. The word might have spread that Pulis' house was still a work in progress for the festival. It would be an understatement to say Mrs. Bagh, and Adhvika don't gel well together. Mrs. Bagh, a tiger pasuman like Adhvika, has been the neighborhood housing committee president since such an organization was formed. It was she herself who formed it. Her husband works for the local government, and she never shied away from using her clout to make life miserable for the residents in that community and all of them feared her, except Adhvika. They all confided in secret with Adhvika about their resentment of Mrs. Bagh, but out in the open, she was their leader.

"Happy Diwali to you too, Mrs. Bagh. What a surprise!" said Adhvika, forcing a stiff smile, hiding the aversion on her face, and letting her in reluctantly.

"We were sent these Rajbhog-Rasgullas from the royal house of Vaibhavapuri. I am sharing this with all of our neighborhood friends. Not everyone would be lucky enough to have these…"

Adhvika stifled her frustration.

"Ah! The royal family and their love for us. We don't like all the attention, but what to do? It just keeps coming our way. Anyways, you should have these. I assure you this is nothing like you have ever tasted before. I just offered it to Aadi and his friend outside. Aadi was overjoyed, and his friend, haha, you should watch his expression, funny guy. I like him. 'It was the best thing he ever had' were his words," said Mrs. Bagh handing the box over to Adhvika.

"Who, Subbu? He has the same enthusiasm describing even drinking water," said Sumati, frowning, without lifting her head and continuing to work on rangoli.

"I don't think you met my friend Sumati here. She is visiting us from Dakshina Vajra Dvipa," said Adhvika.

"Oh, Dear! Nice to meet you. I am Capaweesa…"

"Cup what?" asked Sumati innocently.

"Capaweesa dear…Capaweesa Bagh. It means unique in the Sufarian language. I was born there. *Sufaria.* My dad is Sufarian. My maroon-ish eyes should tell if you notice," said Mrs. Bagh proudly, batting her eyelashes.

"Nice meeting you," said Sumati flatly.

"How do you like Diwali so far? I am sure you don't celebrate it down there where you come from?" said Mrs. Bagh.

"We do—"

"Oh, my bad, But I don't think it is this grand, right?"

"It's very splendid in our regions as well. But it's a bit different in some ways and we don't have people asking weird questions there," said Sumati sternly.

"Different? Oh my…" said Mrs. Bagh innocently, placing her hand on her

chest. "Then how can it be Diwali? You are talking about something else, maybe—"

"Mrs. Capaloosa. Diwali is diverse. By the way, I am Jambu…" cut in Jambu, sensing Sumati might explode any moment now.

"Jambu. It's Cup. Cupppaweesa—not loosa," stressed Sumati.

Adhvika walked into the kitchen muttering, "Hmm, today of all days, she decided to stop by…"

Mrs. Bagh looked around the house without responding to Jambu. "What's up with you, Adhvika, looks like you are still busy preparing for the festival. Hurry up dear, the last I heard Diwali is still today," she said out loud and condescendingly. "Don't tell me now that the festival is next week in this diverse tradition of yours. Haha, just kidding…"

"Here are some sweets." Adhvika came out from the kitchen as if she hadn't heard Mrs. Bagh's words.

"Oh, thank you, dear. So nice of you to offer. My heart aches when I say this, I must decline, though. The entire house is filled with sweets, pastries, cakes, and whatnot from all over the Dvipa. And as if that is not enough, my aunt sent fresh crufflasia shipped from Sufaria. And you know how health conscious I am, I can't accept these anymore. But I acknowledge your intent though…" said Mrs. Bagh sounding gracious and placing her hand on Adhvika's shoulder as if a royal talks to her subject. And she went on, "By the way, that design at the entrance looks interesting…it could use some flowers, though. Doesn't look festive enough."

"It's called kolam—" said Adhvika, slowly standing up, hoping Capaweesa would leave.

"Haha, what a funny name. Do they do this for Diwali? All these new traditions." bellowed Mrs. Bagh interjecting, clapping both her hands.

"Haha, *Capaweesa (you mean)*…? Yes indeed, it is a very funny name…" responded Adhvika in equal vigor, clapping.

Sumati and Jambu stifled their laughter.

Mrs. Bagh's smile changed to resentment as she curled her lips, stood up and said, "Hmm. I must leave now. Have a few more houses to cover. Spreading some festive cheer, all alone. Not many do it anymore, just drag Diwali preparations till the last moment and then complain about lack of time to meet people." She walked hurriedly towards the door, not willing to hear any counter-response.

Adhvika was just glad she was leaving and kept silent, gnashing.

"Oh, I heard you went on a travel. Travel before Diwali? Glad you are back at least for the festival. I was worried you might skip it altogether," said Mrs. Bagh as if she hadn't had enough.

"Don't you worry about me and Diwali, Capaweesa. We celebrate it joyfully with homemade food and accept whatever is given to us gracefully," said Adhvika contemptuously with no more smile on her face.

"Oh! Have your joyful, *gracefully-accepting* festival then and don't forget to pay your dues," said Mrs. Bagh angrily.

"What dues?" Adhvika snapped back.

"You would know if you attended the meeting. The cleaning dues, after Diwali fireworks. The committee decided it will handle the post-festival cleanup of the entire neighborhood this time. I paid on your behalf. The crew will come tomorrow. No fireworks allowed after today."

"When did the meeting happen, and when was this decided?"

"Last Week. My servant Santhu will drop the receipt off tomorrow. It includes the interest." yelled Mrs. Bagh as she left.

"*Interest?* For one week? I was out traveling—*you slimy leecher—*" gritted Adhvika. "She just came to rub it in."

"What a pig!" said Sumati, shaking her head.

Adhvika fumed as she returned to work, "Last year me, Aadi and a few others cleaned up the entire neighborhood promptly the day after Diwali. And she—she was nowhere to be seen. The audacity with which she preaches now...ugh!"

"Don't let her get it into your head," said Jambu.

The bell rang again. Jambu opened the door this time and collected a package.

"It must be the diya. Finally!" said Adhvika in a serious voice.

Chapter 4:

Diwali-like? Not Much

Every year Adhvika has a unique Diwali decor set up as a special attraction. And this time, she decided it was this magical looking brass diya, that she selected after patiently going through many options. An elated Sumati and Adhvika opened the package and took the diya out.

Sumati glared. "How beautiful—"

Cut short by Adhvika's shrieking voice. "*This is not how the diya I ordered looked*—this—this looks different..."

"Different in what way?" asked Sumati.

"I mean, this is totally a different piece. Not the one I ordered," responded Adhvika sternly.

Adhvika dashed inside the bedroom angrily as if to hit someone. Jambu and Sumati looked at each other bewildered.

Meanwhile, Aadi and Subbu completed fixing the lights and announced they were heading out to the market to get some clay diyas and other decorations.

Adhvika called the diya company. Though Diwali was an official holiday, many businesses remained open to cash in the last-minute holiday rush.

"I am so sorry, looks like we have a mix-up. We will mail you the right diya and put it on the fastest shipping possible tomorrow. It should reach you in three days."

"*Three Days? Diwali is today!*" yelled Adhvika.

"Our sincere apologies. Please give us a chance to correct this. And you can keep the one you have now and use it for Diwali. We won't charge for it. We are a small business and had a hectic time this festive—"

"As if I have a choice now," interrupted Adhvika, as she screamed. "*Return my money!*"

"But it's not possible at this moment…"

"So much for all the advertising you did. You spoiled my festive plans," Adhvika lashed out, hung up the phone and sniffed angrily. "I placed this order after confirming every detail, and now they need three more days to send the right one, as if we can reschedule the festival, ha!"

"But this diya is beautiful too…" pacified Jambu. Sumati nodded in agreement. Adhvika, however, looked unconvinced and disappointed. She just went ahead and posted a bad review on the site.

Despite careful confirmation of everything, not only was the shipping delayed and my order, when received, was wrong. They declined to return my money too. I would give zero stars if I could.

There was stark silence in the house. Adhvika was now going with such intensity on the rangoli that it felt like she was going to dig a tile or two. As Sumati was helping Jambu,

"Sumati, can you do the centerpiece? I will help Jambu. I'm almost done here," said Adhvika in a not-so-courteous way. Sumati agreed though she didn't like the tone. The mood just changed in the past hour or so. The negative energy was rubbing off on each other and things got competitive. Sumati wanted to make sure the centerpiece of rangoli came out well. And after a while,

Thuddd...

A noise from outside startled everyone. Sumati and Adhvika rushed outside and saw most of the lights from the roof fell off, and a few were dangling.

Adhvika shook her head disapprovingly. "There goes hours of work futile. Today is not going as planned."

Sumati, who has been very reassuring so far, agreed.

"Err...excuse me, sorry for the intrusion. Can I be of help here?" said a voice nervously. It was Mr. Bolunath Krishnakant. He is a Monkey pasuman. "Couldn't help but notice that all the lights had fallen off. So, I thought, could offer help."

Bolu was a young graduate who moved to this town for a job, days changed to weeks and weeks to months, but he couldn't find the one he was aiming for. So, he picked up a temporary one to make ends meet.

"Sorry, who are you? You don't seem familiar," said Adhvika.

"My mistake. Should have introduced myself first. I am Bolunath, or simply Bolu. I work as a salesman for *Bhujanga Vahana Companies.*"

Though he joined that company thinking it was temporary, destiny was such that he was laid off. So, he no longer worked there. But at that moment, he just lied though he didn't intend to. Actually, it just came out that way.

"I just live across that lake in a tree-house," he said, pointing north. Bolu was homesick and Diwali-sick as well. It's his favorite season. But then, he was too proud to return to his hometown empty-handed. He had a lot of dreams and vowed to return only when he earned some reasonable livelihood. So today, he was walking along the streets, watching all the festivities. He was desperate to be part of something in some fashion. He was never this lonely on Diwali that he could remember.

"So what's in it for you?" asked Adhvika skeptically.

"Nothing. Just fun. Diwali it is..."

"Did you do this before?"

"Not really. But if you can guide..." he responded sheepishly.

Subbu and Aadi were nowhere to be seen. So there was no other option. "Ok. But you have to wait. We have some work to finish inside," said Adhvika hesitantly.

"Or just tell me how you want, I'll do it, and you can go finish your work inside," Bolu replied.

"I have some ideas," said Sumati.

Adhvika gladly let Sumati take over, and she went inside. Sumati gave a rundown of what she had on her mind and then went inside to complete her work. As time progressed, Jambu completed the decorations with Adhvika's help, got dressed for the evening, and started making puja arrangements. Sumati is finishing up on her rangoli. Adhvika went to freshen up. It was almost dusk.

Bolu wrapped up the lights and informed Sumati. She went out to check. The enthusiasm on Sumati's face wore off, "Hmm, these look good...but...hmm...this is not how I explained."

"The—the—lights didn't hold. So I took the liberty to readjust them a bit. Hope it's ok."

Bolu wanted to inform them beforehand, but he remembered they were busy inside. And he just wanted to help in any way he could. So he just decided to fit them the way he thought would be the best.

"Well...good...they look fine...thank you..." murmured Sumati with a half-smile, "I'll let Adhvika know."

Bolu nodded and, for a second, wasn't sure how to react. "Happy Diwali," he said as he walked away disappointed. Sumati went inside. She was confused and didn't feel empowered to thank Bolu wholeheartedly at that moment. She felt she couldn't approve his work without Adhvika's acknowledgment. A lot was going on, and the ripple effect of negative energies was playing on.

The mehendi session was a quickie. No letting the hands dry for six hours, no elaborate designs. Just something simple with a thirty-minute dry-off. Jambu wanted it on too, on the back of his hand. Adhvika and Sumati took turns putting them on each other's hands and then Jambu's. They heard the chatter as Subbu and Aadi finally returned from the market.

"What took you so long?" asked Adhvika sternly.

"It's almost puja time. Where were you?" snarled Sumati.

"Well, look at all we got," replied Aadi pointing to all the bags he and Subbu were carrying.

"Wow, those look like a lot. Did you go on a spending spree?" Sumati gasped.

"Actually, much less than you would ever guess," said Subbu gaily.

"So tell us what happened," asked Jambu curiously.

"While fixing the lights..." said Aadi. "By the way, what happened to the lights outside? Who changed them?" —he just remembered those didn't look how they left.

"They fell off. A stranger called Bolu offered his help and put them back on. Clumsy work you guys did, and then you were off for hours," said Adhvika.

"Oh! Ah, ok. So where was I?" said Aadi. "Yes...As we were fixing lights, neighbor Baburao stopped by."— carefully changing topics realizing where it was leading to.

"He was a delight to talk to and gave many food recommendations. But his best pick this season was the Bunty sweet shop," said Subbu gleefully, "It's newly opened in—"

"Eh?—Sweet shop! Why go to a sweetshop?" Frowned Sumati mouth wide open.

"What else for? Laddoos!" snapped Subbu implying as if it's obvious.

"Poor Adhvika made dozens of dishes and you had to go get laddoos as well," snarled Sumati with hands on her hip and moving her trunk vigorously in circles, implying laddoo. Adhvika nodded in agreement. Her eyes were swollen with emotion.

"More the merrier, I thought," mumbled Subbu sheepishly.

"Ok, ok, let's not get excited. But it was good that we went there," said Aadi with a forced smile, trying to justify. "Let me tell you the actual story. So when Baburao strongly recommended this sweetshop, we decided to try it. Subbu wanted it badly. So we traversed the entire route while stopping at every shop possible for diyas and fireworks. Prices were exorbitant."

"Horrendous, I say—Six clay diyas for twenty varahas? You'll get 2lb rasmalai for that price, better believe," said Subbu shaking his head in disapproval.

"So as we walked and trekked and hiked our way through..." said Aadi poetically.

"Enough of your travel gibberish. You went to the store and got truckloads of sweets, is that it?" Adhvika frowned.

"Woah! What's up with all the anger?" said Aadi leaning back. Subbu put his hand on Aadi's shoulder and swayed his head up and down and then side to side while closing his eyes, comforting Aadi as if to tell him he was not alone in this.

"Okay. So we reached the shop, and here is the twist," continued Aadi.

"I'll tell! I'll tell!" said Subbu. "We went all the way there, and you know what we found out?" Adhvika and Sumati raised their eyebrows, paying attention. Jambu, who was sitting all along, leaned a bit forward keenly.

"Laddoos? Were great. But the pedas were the best in that shop," stressed Subbu, punching the air in excitement. "You got to taste this. You'll love it, Oh! Better believe me."

Sumati clapped her hand on the head and said, "Rama! Rama!" And then started walking straight to the puja room, chanting "*Suklam Baradharam Vishnum Sasivarnam Chaturbhujam.*"— as if she was ready for the puja.

Adhvika put her hands over her head and slouched into the couch. Jambu sighed.

"That is not what I meant when I said a twist," whined Aadi.

Subbu asked, "Well then, what was it?"

At this point, Jambu stood up. "Guys. This is...hmm... Is beginning to test everyone's patience. Is there anything else you want to share? Or let's all get ready for puja now?"

"Err—Ok—I'll be quick," said Aadi. "At the sweet shop, we overheard people talking about the stores beyond the main temple that

sold diyas and other things for reasonable prices. So we went all the way there."

Adhvika pretended to close her eyes but was listening. Sumati turned back and waited to give them one more chance.

"Wow, main temple? That's a ways off," said Jambu.

"Yes. But we did not buy anything there."

"Hmm," grunted Jambu, sounding edgy.

"Ok—ok, we crossed the temple, passing by all the stores. While prices were much better, we kept going until we reached this store on the corner, not much visible from the main street and not many customers in it. As such, the day was soon about to end. The old shopkeeper was desperate. That allowed us to strike a great bargain," explained Aadi proudly.

"Yes, he was offering six diyas for only twelve varahas. I bargained it for ten," gloated Subbu. "And then Aadi was fabulous. We wanted to get eighteen diyas, so we asked him for a further discount."

"Yes, with some reluctance, he took three varahas off and offered eighteen diyas for twenty-seven. But we asked him to round it off to twenty-five," said Aadi.

"And then he resisted, well, you bet, we resisted too. And Aadi had a brilliant plan," said Subbu prodding him. "He winked at me to pretend to walk out, which we did. And that shopkeeper called us back and gave us the deal. We knew he was desperate, eighteen diyas for just twenty-five varahas. Can you believe it?"

"And then we got some fireworks and akasa deepas. That would be a whole story by itself. Since you all have been so grouchy, I'll spare you the details. But we got it all together for a grand total of just seventy-five varahas. *Boo Yaa!* Now you tell us, are you mad that we got late?" said Aadi in a demanding tone.

"Would it have been like one hundred and seventy-five or more if we just bought it here in our town? We saved at least hundred varahas, " exclaimed Subbu.

"So you basically haggled the heck out of a hapless seller?" bemoaned Jambu.

"Oh, Jambu! Don't be so dramatic," said Aadi.

"There were literally no customers. We helped him," said Subbu.

"We are getting close to muhurta time. Quick! Let's get ready," said Sumati.

"Hand me the bags, and I'll start setting up the diyas," said Adhvika.

"Ok, we will take that as a thank you for a great job done," said Aadi sarcastically as they all were pumped up for Diwali night.

Chapter 5:

Deliberation

"How about this blue kurta?"

"Blue doesn't suit me; I like the yellow one."

"Wow, this saree looks so beautiful with the bright red color and that contrast on the border..."

"Yes indeed. But I wore it for this Dussehra. I'll go with that green lehenga. Look, this one with its pink and yellow color combination looks so majestic..."

Chitter chatter permeated from inside the bedrooms. Jambu was walking up and down the hallway restlessly. It was bothering him. He wanted to say something but didn't want that to be direct and imposed, but rather something convincing and that triggered a thought. He always believed in paving the way rather than forcing something.

Quick, can't waste much time. It is already getting dusky outside, he thought. He collected and tried to talk but couldn't get his voice out. "Arr...Ahem," he cleared his throat and tried to speak out loudly for the rest of them to hear—"Alright, it's time for me to head out!"—he said as half of it came out in a hoarse whisper—"Arr...ahem," he cleared his throat again.

"Yes, we will head out shortly after the puja," replied Adhvika.

"I can't wait for the (fire) crackers!" happy-squealed Sumati.

"I mean," he grumbled, "I am going out to celebrate Diwali," he half-shouted. No response from the other side. *Ugh! That is not what I wanted to say anyways. Okay, let me try again,* he said to himself and took a long breath.

"I am leaving now. Thanks for making me part of the festive celebrations!" yelled Jambu, cupping hands around his mouth. He shouted as if he was announcing to a hundred people standing a hundred feet away.

"Is it Jambu?"

"Looks like he is in some pain."

"Jambu, are you ok?"

Everyone came running to the hallway, startled. "Jambu, what happened? Are you ok? We heard a scream!" said Aadi with a stunned face.

"Oh! My apologies, didn't mean to startle you!" said Jambu embarrassingly, realizing he said it much louder than he wanted it to be. "I was heading out, thought I would let you know. Have a happy Diwali."

Questions followed—

"Heading out! Where to?"

"What for?"

"I thought you would stay here for the night."

"Today is Diwali. To celebrate it," said Jambu facing the doorway without looking back.

"Eh! Then what are we doing here? Holi?" asked Adhvika, screwing her face up.

"I mean, to celebrate in its true sense," said Jambu, waving his hand.

"Enough of these riddles. Can you be more direct?" said Subbu in a mildly frustrated voice.

"Alright! Alright!" said Jambu. Turning back, taking a deep breath, he asked, "What is Diwali?"

"There he goes..." said Subbu, shaking his head.

"Festival of Lights!" said Sumati sharply.

"Ah! Lights as in what?"

"Light up the diyas, fireworks. What else?" snapped Sumati with a puzzled look. "Oh! We did not light up our house yet, is that it?"

"No, No! Why are we celebrating Diwali? The importance of it?"

"Oh! I know it. Long long ago, very long ago, Lord Rama went on a mission to find Sita Maa. He traveled and—" went on Aadi in his narrative style.

"Hmm! I am not asking for the reason behind it. But—"

They started becoming restless and were in no mood to engage in Jambu's enigma-ridden questionnaire.

"Jambu did we miss the muhurta for the puja?" wondered Adhvika interrupting Jambu. Her body language was pleading with him to come to the point already.

"Diwali means festivities, celebrations, feasting…" said Subbu as if it was his final leap attempt to give it all he got.

"Yes…Yes, but—"

"Ah! Now I got you, Jambu. Feasting, yes! We've been so busy today that we forgot the simple joy of sitting together and relishing these delicacies that Adhvika has put so much effort into making," Subbu blabbered. He didn't listen to Jambu, who was trying to engage him. Jambu nodded to indicate no. That was not what he was asking.

"All I am asking is, what is the true essence of Diwali? What does it teach us? The meaning behind it!" shouted Jambu again, as if it was his last attempt to find the answer he was looking for.

"Good over evil!" snapped Sumati in equal volume.

"Yes!" clapped Jambu. "That is what I was looking for."

"You could have asked that directly," said Adhvika, slouching forward.

"Err…I was trying to…" mumbled Jambu sheepishly.

"Hope over despair!" said Aadi loudly, with his chest sticking out.

"Light over darkness!" said Adhvika passionately.

"Yes. Yes. That is correct," said Jambu with a quivering voice, emotionally swaying his head, the emotion that one feels when enormous patience pays off, the kind of emotion animals in savannah feel when it rains after a drought of six months—"Goodness, positivity, light, hope...in whose lives...?" he questioned in a whispering voice while extending both his hands, his pupils dilated, feeling glad that he is finally zeroing in on the point.

"In everyone's livesss...!"

Sumati gasped, Adhvika shrieked, Aadi shivered, and Jambu's emotion evaporated.

"Why did you scream like that?" asked Aadi.

"Err. Well, you all had your turn yelling. I thought it was mine now," shrugged Subbu as if it was obvious.

"Great! Everyone's lives," said Jambu, quickly collecting and returning to the topic. "While we can only hope and wish the light, positivity, and goodness are spread in everyone's lives and we for sure yearn for it to be in the ones we love the most, our families and dearest friends, shouldn't it at the very least also be in the people we had an opportunity to interact with today?"

Everyone nodded.

"And let alone hoping to spread the light, what if we become the reason for stopping it?" Jambu paused, hoping they all got what he was pointing to.

"We? How?" questioned Sumati.

"In the ones we interacted with today," added Jambu as if that would make everything apparent.

"You better not be referring to the shopkeeper episode when you say that!" Frowned Subbu.

"Don't be so angry. Breathe..." said Jambu, taking a deep breath.

"Breathe? *My laddoo!*" said Subbu looking further agitated. *It's almost dusk. It's time for festive joy, puja is yet to be done, and the smells of the foods are making my tummy grumble. I could hear all the Diwali cheer from the neighborhood, and here is Jambu holding up everything by spreading the epitome of boredom with his laborious lecture. My laddoo!* thought Subbu. Typical Subbu, his emotions always come in abundance.

"But Jambu, we struck a bargain with an adult in full cognizance. We forced no one's hand." Waved off Aadi.

"We are no cheats!" scoffed Subbu with raised eyebrows.

"Oh, dear Subbu. Don't be so extreme. I never said that. Nor did you force anyone. But it seemed you took advantage of a very desperate person. Which is what we are discussing here."

"Ah! Don't be so dramatic, Jambu. The prices were outrageous to start with. You would sell off your clothes and stand in undergarments if you entertained these opportunists," argued Aadi.

"But were they?" continued Jambu. "Were they at the place where you bought these? Wasn't this particular shopkeeper, at least, beyond reasonable?"

"We provided business to an otherwise empty store. That is no darkness in my books," stressed Subbu.

"Yet you worked your way to pay much lower than the worth of the goods. You didn't spread any darkness but did simmer down whatever hope was left," said Jambu.

"This old man, not having customers, how is it our problem? He probably would have quoted a higher price on a good day," said Aadi.

"I also gave some pedas to his little girl. Don't make us the evil here," said Subbu.

"My intention is not that. Also, I don't propose you pay over what you can afford. That would not be wise, either. You are good, hardworking people and I respect that. And what that old man would have done on a good day is unknown to me. But today, given all the facts here, he was being very fair in his offering, much better than we could ever expect, yet you decided to stretch it further and take undue advantage of his situation. What the other shopkeepers tried to do to you, you did the same to him and even worse, don't you think?"

"Hmm..." groaned Subbu.

"When you put it that way, it kind of sounds...hmm...bad. But you assume he was hapless as if it's a given. While it did come across that way to us, we don't know that for sure. Just in case, what if he had a very busy day and was just looking to offload the rest of the goods quickly as it was towards the end of the day?" said Aadi with a deep ponder.

"True. In that case, thankfully, the result of your action wouldn't be that grim. Yet the act by itself is still questionable, isn't it? I'll leave it to you to reflect and gauge if this is worth it," Jambu said thoughtfully. "But if that was not the case, then this shopkeeper, who is old per you— has a little girl and is having a bad day with his business in what has already been a very difficult time for everyone. And then...what would have been an already meager sale was further cut short. All of this goes against everything Diwali stands for."

"We just got caught up in the moment. We weren't thinking," said

Aadi, "All this money we saved today wouldn't matter much in the big picture anyways." —as he was thankful that they were doing okay and the tough times hadn't affected them.

"Saving is not the issue, but how we do that matters," said Adhvika.

Jambu Nodded.

Toooooot...tooottt. Tooottt...toottt...toottt...
Toooooot...tooottt. Tooottt...toottt...toottt...

Sumati was concerned, Adhvika was confused, Aadi was astonished, and Jambu was puzzled.

"Subbu are you ok?" asked Adhvika.

"What happened?" questioned Sumati.

"How will...hu...hu...how will the poor little girl celebrate Diwali now...*tooooottttt*...Just two pedas won't cut it," bawled Subbu wiping his tears.

Jambu continued to look at Subbu curiously, wondering if he was the same person that was thundering like a storm just two minutes prior. He was not new to Subbu's emotions, but each time it astonished him the same, if not more.

"Let's go fix that now Subbu," comforted Aadi.

"Adhvika," said Jambu, quickly coming back to the topic, "I understand the fault lies with the diya seller you were angry with, but it seemed she tried to make amends honestly." He was referring to the phone conversation she had earlier that day.

"Hmm. Yes, yes, she did. I wasn't myself. The interaction with Capaweesa and then the tiredness of the trip all piled up, and I burst out at that moment. But I must admit the seller went above and beyond in her attempt to get the issue corrected. I have some fixing to do now. It's been on the back of my mind, but I was trying to evade it," said Adhvika in a repentant tone.

"I have something to say," said Sumati guiltily. "I didn't thank Mr. Bolu properly."

"Bolu?" asked Aadi.

"The guy who helped us fix the lights while you were gone," replied Adhvika.

"Oh! Why didn't you, Sumati?" snapped Aadi, bringing the discussion back to Sumati. He didn't want to revisit the lights episode.

"I was preoccupied with multiple things," said Sumati. "And it was very insensitive of me—"

"I think I rubbed off my pressure on Sumati," interjected Adhvika apologetically.

"Ah! No worries, both of you. *Tooot*...We—We all have some fixing to do then," said Subbu, hoarsely still recovering from the bawling he did.

"I didn't bring this up to make you all feel terrible," said Jambu, stretching his hands to the front as if it was his conclusion speech, and he had to give it now. "We all sometimes get carried away in our daily endeavors and fail to grasp our actions and words' consequences on others...While the expectation isn't to scrutinize every step of ours, but if there is a chance to reflect on our actions, we should do it," he said sanctimoniously.

Holding his hands behind his back and ambling away from them, he continued, "And...and in that process, if we do realize, indeed, there was a wrongful act that we knowingly/unknowingly perpetrated, we surely must do everything in our disposal to set it right."

Turning back, facing them and waving his right hand, "At times..." he hissed—"At times, despite self-reflection, we might yet not recognize the unjust endeavors that we may have unknowingly committed and carry on with our business as usual. On such occasions…"—he gave a careful pause and looked all around to make sure they were attentive —"on such occasions,"—he continued while raising his finger, indicating this is very important—"if we are fortunate enough, then our dear friends, family or well-wishers might have made a note of such ventures and pointed us to such a misrecognized act of potential wrongdoing," he carefully observed.

"You should then rethink, discern and rectify it if needed," he said, nodding his head. "But…but whatever you decide to do, make sure you are true and good to your heart in making such a decision and not letting your ego misguide," he warned. "Repentance is no shame," he grunted. "In the end, if all follow this simple mantra, the world would be a better place," he choked with emotion. "Kudos!" he exclaimed. "Kudos to all of you, on this auspicious Deepavali day, for keeping your egos aside and acknowledging the problem and now on the mission to ameliorate it… kudos…" he declared. "That's all, that's all I wanted to say."

Pheeeeeeeezzzzzzz…

Subbu blew his trunk and said, "Jambu, other than kudos, I didn't understand much. What exactly are you trying to explain?"

"Ah! Thank goodness I wasn't the only one not following," replied Aadi.

"I understand that Jambu is happy about something. He said kudos thrice," said Adhvika in a confirming voice.

"I also heard Diwali once but was concerned when Jambu started with the word terrible. In the end, it didn't seem that bad though," said Sumati trying to make sense.

"Err…I meant today…hmm…you know what, all I was saying is

good luck to you all. And Sumati, I will help you to find Bolu," replied Jambu.

Aadi ran outside. Subbu was about to follow him but turned back and grabbed a box of sweets that he put on the table. "No laddoos, no Diwali," he grinned.

"Subbu, wait!" said Adhvika as she went inside and brought a container bowl. "Here is fruit custard. You mentioned there was a little girl. Little kids love this."

"You're the best! '' said Subbu before heading out to catch up to Aadi, and off they went on a hunt to find the old shopkeeper's place.

Adhvika decided to call back the diya seller. She hoped they were still open while Jambu and Sumati went to look for Bolu.

Chapter 6:

Let There Be Light

When Adhvika was looking for what she imagined would be a beautiful-looking centerpiece, a newly put-up online-only store was the last one on her mind. She went from store to store physically to find something that could accentuate her home's festive decorations but could find nothing to her liking. And then the trip happened. Just for this year, she thought she could go easy on the decorations. But could she? No, not her. So she continued looking online while on the trip until she landed on what she called the magical brass diya in a random search. But there was a problem, not many reviews at all. Could she trust this seller? The products looked truly good, though. So she decided to call the seller nevertheless, which helped her ease into the decision. The person she spoke to was very courteous and helped alleviate all her concerns. *Mighty impressive*, thought Adhvika at that time, and the rest was history.

H. Harin Crafts and Artifacts was the store, named after its owner and founder Hima Harin, a gazelle pasuman. Hima was one of the very few girls from her remote town who was educated and the only one with a graduate degree. She worked at a day job until she decided to quit to pursue her passion for handicrafts and grew her part-time hobby into a small business. Started with some long-time friends and residents from her native town and built products that they could sell online, eliminating the middle layer. Then, created her own company, hired a few more and turned it into a regular business. And now, she is on the quest to expand it to physical stores and even sell them to other vendors. The actual people behind the products always get the profit share. That is the motto of the company.

"You are an inspiration, Hima! Thank you for sharing your story on such a happy day," said Adhvika. When she called the company, Hima was the one who answered the phone, the last one working, wrapping up for the day. And as Adhvika initiated the conversation, unintentionally, the conversation delved into Hima's personal story.

"But currently, we are struggling. Formalizing my business and taking it online resulted in its explosion, but it has its downside. Short-staffed, working overtime and the resulting burnout. It's been difficult to find people who have the passion and are not just looking for quick money, and as a fallout this festive season, we have had some mix-ups. Nevertheless, none of these will or should matter to the end customer. It's my fault, period! I have some lessons to learn. My apologies again," said Hima.

"Ah! You are so hard on yourself. The way you dealt with the mix-up and your outdone attempts to compensate for it, it's like no other that I have seen. My apologies. Rage has overtaken my judgment earlier. I wanted to tell you that this diya is very beautiful as well. Thanks for letting me keep this; I want to pay for it. And also no rush on the original one. Keep up the good work!"

Hima was delighted and moved. She did not want to take any money for the trouble caused.

"Sometimes words give more comfort than any money. Thank you for the encouragement. We needed it the most today."

"But I wouldn't feel right if I didn't pay. Kindly send me the invoice," insisted Adhvika.

"Thank you!" said Hima after a few seconds of silence. "Glad to end my workday on a high note. Time to go to celebrate with my family. Wish you a very happy Diwali!"

"Happy Diwali to you and your family

too!" wished Adhvika and hung up. She went ahead and modified the review she posted earlier to something positive. Gave it five stars.

Sumati and Jambu were on the lookout for finding Bolu. All that Sumati remembers is his name and that he lived across the lake in a tree-house. As they started to circumvent the lake, the presence of moving life became sparser. Most of the other side has been wood until recently. And as the city expanded, new neighborhoods sprung up, but they haven't been completely developed yet. As Jambu and Sumati reached the other side, it became somber and quieter. The distance between each house was now equal to ten houses on their side. The huge light decorations and giant rangolis in front of the houses made up for what otherwise seemed to be a very toned-down and intimate celebration. Not a single pasuman to be seen. It seemed as if only people who preferred a very private life lived there.

Aadi and Subbu were on a similar mission on the other side of the city. But unlike Sumati and Jambu, they found help. They went jet-speed to the shopkeeper's store that they had visited earlier. From there started making inquiries about him and got some pointers on his whereabouts. Accordingly, they entered a town that personified Diwali celebrations as they went further. It was called *Bhinnatva Nagari*—situated on the outskirts of the city. All sorts of stories and folktales about this place and a mere mention of it invited exciting and passionate debates. Aadi himself heard a lot about it but hadn't gotten a chance to visit it before. And here they are on their first adventure into Bhinnatva Nagari.

They moved along ever-winding narrow streets with cramped buildings with floors on top of each other. Some of the buildings looked crooked or squished and, in a few cases, both. And in between these buildings, there were shops of all sizes. Diwali here has been the most boisterous yet. Diyas all along, kids screaming and jumping on the roads, people bursting fireworks from balconies, firing rockets from the terrace, wishing each other, running across the streets not minding a bit about the vehicles, the shops bustling with last-minute activity, colorful garlands everywhere, glittering lights all along and the vehicles somehow traversing through all this commotion. "Diwali Shubhechha!" wished a woman waving her hands, leaning from the first-floor balcony to her neighbor. "Diwali Ni Shubhkamna!" shouted another. *Diwali aavi,sathe ghani khushiyon laavi*...a song coming from a speaker. Passing half a mile distance here felt like ten miles as the crowds were huge. The language changed rapidly every few meters. *Deepavali Valthukkal!* They saw a huge banner hanging over the middle of the road. A Group of girls were busy giving finishing touches to the kolams in front of their houses which ended right on the road. "Deepam Vilakethu," someone shouted. As Aadi and Subbu stopped by a snacks shop to ask for further directions. "Please, come in sir. Dayacheyandi, Deepavali Subhakankshalu! Panduga specials. Pootharekulu, gavvalu, palakova, murukulu..." The shop owner started reading through the list. Subbu and Aadi politely refused and quickly asked for directions and left. Subbu was stunned they were selling pootharekulu in this part of the Dvipa. *I should visit this later*, he thought. The buildings were dazzling with lights as if they were constructed from them.

The tri-festive season gives us a reason to be happy and jolly as *Deepavali* — read a sign board. *Plum cakes and pastries, festive specials* read another.

They were circumventing a huge Banyan tree with a raised platform around it. The tree was decorated with lights and a lot of deepas on the platform surrounding it. On closer observation, the deepas were arranged so that they read *Deepotsavam Ashamsakal.*

Aadi was gazing at the tree with his mouth wide open and taking in the sights. He said, "How beautiful—"

"*Watch out!*" screamed Subbu as rowdy youngsters set off the

firecrackers on the road and ran away.

"*I am! I am!*" assured Aadi, shaking it off and becoming alert.

As they further moved along, the lights were hung from one side of the road to the other: flashy and blinking. *Shubh Deepavali*, a sign made of lights, hung in the air in the middle of the road with *Shubh Laabh* signs just below it. Finally, the winding road paved into a T-crossing junction. They stopped at the last house before the crossing as they saw people out, celebrating.

Diwali ki dher sari shubhkamnaayein...Mu meeta karo...

People wished each other as youngsters touched the feet of elders to take blessings. Elders gave money and gifts to kids.

"Happy Diwali! What can I help you with?" asked one of the residents.

"Happy Diwali to you, too!" said Aadi and Subbu as they asked for directions.

"Ah! The main center shopkeepers, most of them live in Bose colony. Go back a few meters and take the first left. Go along the curved road, skip the first two turns, and take the third right, around the arts and culture center building. You can ask someone there who should be able to help."

Meanwhile, Sumati and Jambu finally reached the tree-house colony. They all looked newly built, many of them not occupied. They asked a few people if they knew Bolu, but none seemed to know. With disappointment, they head back. *That might be the reason Bolu was roaming in their part of the neighborhood earlier that day for some festive fervor as this area looked mostly empty*, they both thought.

Back at Bhinnatva Nagari, Aadi and Subbu continued their quest. Traffic was crawling along. Diwali was at its peak glory now. *When would they reach back home at this pace*, they both wondered. On the right, a group of pasumans were covering their head with a cloth in reverence

56

and entering a building that read *Diwali langar*. Similar sights are a bit further on the left. A long line of impoverished pasumans patiently waiting for their turn to have food in front of a temple with a sign that read *E jagadalli Annadaana-Deepavali special. Dashain-Tihar ko Subhakamana, tri-festive sale*, said a signboard in front of a big mall further along.

"How do people even communicate with each other with such diversity?" asked Subbu in amazement.

"Just like how we have interacted with them so far. A bit of our native tongue, throwing a few common words that cut across the languages and mixing some sign language into it, should be good enough," replied Aadi. Finally, after a very engulfing journey, they approached a tall building with a big banner that read *Shubo Kali Pujo - Shubo Dipaboli*. It was covered with huge garlands and paper decor. It was the arts and culture center. They took a right immediately after as instructed and found a directional sign that said, *Bose colony 250 meters ahead*.

That was intense. Three miles felt like an eternity. It was one heck of a Bhinnatva Nagari—the town of diversity indeed, they thought. Now that the traffic was less, they drove fast, and finally, the narrow road led to a mud path until it reached a dead end with a big sign archway that read *Bose colony-since 1923*. Diyas flickering on both sides of the arch mounts. Things looked much simmered down in Bose colony. Few mud houses, some huts, some flickering diyas here and there. They were told exactly where the old shopkeeper lived. They reached a gloomy-looking hut with thatched roof, a bit disconnected from the hustle and bustle of the festive night. It was dark, with the only light source being the streetlight at the corner. Aadi and Subbu slowly approached the house and knocked on the door. The old shopkeeper opened the door and recognized them but looked puzzled, wondering why they were here.

Aadi smiled and said, "Sorry to disturb you at this hour. But we came to pay our dues."

"What dues?" asked the baffled shopkeeper.

"Let us explain," continued Aadi. "We didn't feel a fair bargain was struck earlier today. We underpaid you for the quality and quantity of the items we got. We wanted to stick to the original price, hence pay you the remaining amount."

The shopkeeper let them inside the hut and introduced himself as Shyam Lal and the little kid was his granddaughter, Minnu. They were sheep pasumans. The hut was small, with only one room, a cord-woven cot, a small mattress on the floor, a couple of blankets and a stove on the other side. That's about it. There were some boxes in the corner across the main door, all jumbled one on top of another.

"Not to deviate from the conversation, but is there a reason for total lack of festivities here?" wondered Subbu.

A dejected-looking Shyam Lal took a deep breath and said, "Festivities hmm…It's been a very tough season. We are hardly able to make ends meet. There are still many unsold products that took a lot of effort to make, some of them stored there." Pointing to those boxes in the corner. "Nevertheless, we plan to have a small gathering on the street near the colony temple and let the kids play. That's it for this Diwali."

Aadi paid the remaining amount and offered some more. Shyam Lal politely refused the extra money. "We want to buy a few more items," said Subbu, winking at Aadi. Aadi nodded in agreement, appreciating Subbu's thought of helping Shyam Lal.

They got all the items Shyam Lal had stored in his house and paid him. "Oh! I almost forgot, here is fruit custard," said Subbu. "Do you like laddoos? Have them as well." He offered them to Minnu. Her eyes filled with excitement, and she stepped forward. Aadi immediately took some money, put it on the custard bowl and nudged it towards Minnu.

"I thank you for your benevolence, but I cannot accept—" said Shyam Lal.

Aadi cut in, "But it is Diwali tonight—"

"And you made our Diwali much brighter by coming to pay the remaining money and everything else you bought here. Please, I can't—"

"But Shyam ji...We haven't given our Diwali gift to the kid yet. And without doing that, how can we leave?" said Aadi as he took a diya out of the boxes he bought, looked at Minnu and asked if she wanted to light it. She jumped in excitement and looked at her grandfather. He smiled in return with a slight nod. Subbu and Aadi helped the girl light the diya.

"Let there be light," said Aadi emotionally. They gave the custard bowl and some money to Minnu and started decorating the house with the diyas and akasa deepas they had just got. Shyam Lal wasn't comfortable.

"You already did so much for us," he bemoaned.

"This is nothing, Shyam ji. The price you sold us all these for is much below the market offering," said Subbu insistingly, showing both the bags in his hands. "Moreover, we get to decide what gift to give. Isn't it? Please let us do it this time."

The hut soon began to beam with Diwali Kanti. Minnu was elated and started jumping up and down and clapping. Shyam Lal was happy in tears that his little granddaughter could celebrate the festival in its full glory. And as they went out, the neighborhood kids gathered around. Aadi and Subbu distributed the laddoos, leftover diyas and other items they bought. One of the neighbors lit up the sparklers and flowerpots. *Diwali ki bahut badhai ho...Happy Diwali*, they all wished each other and just like that, the neighborhood was spread with festivities. Shyam Lal thanked Aadi and Subbu profusely for their benignity, which they humbly declined. They were more than glad that they decided to come to pay their dues on that very night and not think about pushing it to another day. The light they witnessed in Minnu's eyes had no equivalence to anything else they experienced that day. They finally bid goodbye to Shyam Lal and Minnu and rushed back home. They took an alternate route, as suggested by Shyam Lal, escaping traffic. As much as they wanted to relive the stunning chaos and exuberance of Bhinnatva Nagari, they had no time. Sumati and Jambu returned home to an awaiting Adhvika, and later Subbu and Aadi were back.

Chapter 7:

Love, Light, and Happiness

The bliss that Subbu and Aadi felt inside for making Minnu's Diwali happen sent them into a zone of transcendence. As soon as they reached home, Aadi walked straight to Jambu, held both his hands and started swaying in a slow dance.

"Oh dear Jambu, what can we give you, fortunate to have you as our dearest friend-uuuu...Oh dear Jambuuuuu," he howled and growled discordantly.

Subbu took over and continued the dance with Jambu, "Thank you! Oh dear Jambu, because of you we met Shyam Lal and Minnu-uu...Oh Dear Jambuuuuu," singing even more inharmoniously.

"Who are they?" asked Adhvika.

"The shopkeeper and the little one, his granddaughter," stated Subbu in an obvious tone.

"We not only paid our dues and gave the custard to Minnu. We celebrated Diwali there. You must meet that little one. She is so full of life," jumped Aadi.

"That sounds awesome! And I—I spoke to Hima Harin, the owner of the store that I bought the brass diya from," Adhvika narrated her story. "Oh my, her story is like Diwali light! Thank you, Jambu, for that push. I needed that to make a call to her."

Aadi turned around, facing Jambu eye to eye, "Oh Jambu, you opened our eyes to real Diwali today," he said as he pulled his whiskers back, turned Jambu's head to the side and *tsupppttttmuaaahhhhhh!!!!* Kissed him on the cheek.

"Uh—oh—err—I mean—well—haha—huh—ho—ahem—so..." wobble-talked Jambu as he turned pink with happy-blushy-awkward-embarrassment. "I just—discussed—didn't do much...you flatter—I need some water," he said walking towards the kitchen table. Of all the appreciation Jambu had ever received, this was a tad bit...well—actually—way too much for him.

"Hmm...But I couldn't find Bolu, though," said gloomy-looking Sumati.

"Who is Bolu now—err—I think I know," muttered Aadi wasting no time to realize it's a topic best not touched.

"Oh my rasmalai...dear, don't you worry," consoled Subbu holding Sumati's face in his arms.

"We will find Bolu...that I promise you," said Adhvika.

"Ahem! Sumati, don't be so hard on yourself," said Jambu, recovering from the great flattering fiasco he just encountered and more confident than ever to deliver his typical speech. "Sometimes the outcome evades...despite veracious, tenacious efforts and never it had been so true than to keep the spirits high in such circumstances, no matter how much so-ever dismayed they might be," he roared. "It's not as if a horrendous mistake was perpetrated," he sighed.

"Eh!" said Sumati as everyone along with her looked perplexed.

"My laddoo. I didn't get a single word of it," mumbled Subbu.

"Err—I meant. You truly felt remorseful and gave your best shot to correct the mistake. That's all that matters, don't beat yourself up," said Jambu.

Everyone nodded. "We better get ready for puja now," reminded Adhvika.

They all got dressed up at their dazzling best. Adhvika lit up the diyas in the puja room, as Jambu prepared everything needed for the rituals. They have only one thing to do before starting the puja: light up the house. Adhvika lit up the brass diya and placed some clay diyas along the boundaries of the main rangoli. Jambu put the lit up diyas along the corners of the walls in the hallway. Sumati decorated the kolam outside the house with deepas, one in the center, the rest in a circle all along the border and then she put two of them, one on either side of the entrance door and one on either side of the entrance gate as well. Aadi and Subbu switched on the lights outside the house and the ones all along the walls in the hallway and put a few more diyas all along the outside porch wall. They hung akasa deepas along the corners of the porch roof. They all entered the puja room as the house got decked up and shined in its full Diwali prakasa light. It was way past the muhurta time, but they took happiness and solace in the fact that the actual muhurta gadiyas were used for a greater cause that truly reflected the essence of the festival.

Om Sri Maha Lakshmiyei Namah...

Puja has begun. The room reverberated with Mantras and Stotras that Jambu was reciting. The rest sat on the floor around the puja place with hands in Anjali Mudra, inferring reverence and Bhakti.

As the Mantras chanting continued, the presiding deity was offered flowers and Naivedya. Perhaps for the first time in the day, there were no wandering thoughts in their mind, no pressing concerns, no restlessness, nothing they yearned for or resented, as for the next many minutes, they sat there completely surrendered to the positive energy that engulfed the room. A sense of serenity prevailed, with only peace and joy in everyone's mind.

Eventually, as the puja ended with Aarti, the rings of Ghanta and blessings, they all recited their prayers, bowed with humility—called *sashtanga pranama*, in front of the presiding deity and consumed the prasada thereafter.

"Sarve Janah Sukhino Bhavantu!" concluded Jambu.

It doesn't matter how Diwali had been so far, frustrations-misses-disappointments or jubilant-happiness-celebrations; but there came that point akin to kids and elders, kings and peasants, friends and foes when they let loose and just immerse themselves in the best the night had to offer yet. That's the fireworks time. The crisp autumn nightly breeze made the flickering diyas look even more beautiful. The Pulis, Gajas, and Jambu were in high spirits as they cracked jokes on each other, pulled each other's leg, and bellowed songs. And there stood Adhvika in adoration of the rangoli and the brass diya that accentuated the beauty of everything else.

"Oh, this beautiful colorful rangoli...reminds me of Holi," said Adhvika.

"It's not Holi, you silly. Today is Deepavali," nudged Sumati. And then they burst into a song...

Beautiful rangolis, as colorful as Holi.
Wonder what the occasion? It's Deepavali.

The sights of flickering diyas and the akasa deepas...
What else to expect? It's Deepavali.

Sounds of bustling markets, bright and shiny fireworks,
Fret not! Just sing along. It's Deepavali.

The tri-festive season, gives us a reason
to be happy and jolly as Deepavali.

As streets are decorated, with lights and floral garlands,

Eclectic styles of mehendi, adorn our very hands.

Family, friends, kids and elders, get together and cheer along!

The festive feasts are almost ready! Why wait? Bring them on.

As you get all beamy, lest you forget the needy.
Carry the essence of Deepavali.

Love, light, happiness...shun the worldly meanness.
Let it always be known as Deepavali.
Wishing everyone a sparkling Deepavali...

"Just two bags? We should have got more. These will be done in no time," said Aadi, disappointedly looking at the bags with fireworks.

"Those are more than enough," said Jambu, "The idea is to enjoy the festival, not abuse it—"

"Hand them to me," said Subbu as if he had had enough of a discussion.

"First me!" cried Aadi.

"Not before me," ran Jambu grabbing one of the bags as they all squabbled.

Meanwhile, Adhvika and Sumati quietly set off some fireworks from the other bag.

Rock paper scissors—

"Aha! Subbu, you are out."

Rock paper scissors—

"Jambu, you are out. I won!" thumped Aadi. "I told you it would always be me first with the fireworks."

"I love flowerpots," said Adhvika as she lit four of them in a row.

"Hmm, which one should I do first?" asked Aadi, examining the bag seriously.

"Ugh. Doesn't matter. Maybe the flowerpots?" shrugged Subbu.

"Hmm, flowerpots are for kids and…Adhvika…and Sumati," waved Aadi dismissively. "Ahh! This moon fountain. First, it would jitter jatter effusing beautiful fire sparkles like a flowerpot, then it would pause and splutter, flutter cracking sounds with bustling fire."

"Sounds good. Go ahead," nudged Subbu.

"What fun in just one. I'll light three of them side by side," said Aadi gleamingly.

"There are only three in this bag. Leave one for me."

"Well, a deal is a deal. Winners get to choose." Smirked Aadi cheekily, prodding Subbu.

"Aghh…Do one first, do anything at all," grunted Jambu.

Sumati lit up three bhoo-chakras in the meantime. Adhvika and she were doing a little hopping jig dance over the fire sparkles emitting from it.

"Be careful, Sumati. Your Saree!" shrieked Adhvika.

"No worries," exclaimed Sumati. "This is so much fun."

"Guys, look here!" screeched Adhvika. "Come join us."

"Ah! Just that? Now look what I am going to do here," said Aadi haughtily as Subbu and Jambu stood there impatiently.

"One here…" Aadi took three steps to the side "Second one here…Third one here. Guys, is this distance ok?"

"Dude, it's fine. Just light up something for Diwali's sake, my laddoo!" snarled Subbu.

Aadi put all three side by side with three step distance between them. "Ok, it's time to light them," he teased.

"Uffff!" sighed Subbu.

Dammm-Doommm..

damamamamamamadoommomodmdomdamamdododommom....

Aadi jumped back with fear, startled by the sound of a huge ladi. "Ahh, these damn bombs and ladis. What's up with these people? Are they mind-numbingly deaf or what? To set off such high decibel ones. Should I go to reason with them?" growled Jambu.

"Phew! Ok, I am lighting them now," said Aadi in a hurry going back to the moonshots he placed side-by-side.

"Guys look at these," cried Sumati rapturously. Adhvika and she were holding bustling Vishnuchakras. Jambu joined them and started having fun.

"Ok, here you go..." said Aadi.

"Alright, that one looks lit, now move to the next one. Come on," yelled Subbu.

"Yes, yes, doing it. There you go, number two, now the third."

"Move a bit forward. You are barely touching them. The second one is not lit yet."

"Oh, ok." Aadi went back to the previous one.

"The first one will go off any moment now!"

"Oh my!" said Aadi as he jumped and fell flat on his back. He got up, dusted himself and speed-walked back with a nervous smile. "Haha. Let's just enjoy one at a time."

They waited and waited, and the first one went...

..................*tusssss...*

"Is it still lit?" wondered Aadi.

"Doesn't seem so," said Jambu gawking at it with an open mouth through his glasses.

"I am going to light up those leaves and call it a Diwali bonfire now if you don't let me take over," groaned Subbu, throwing his hands up.

"Ok, the last attempt. Let me light the first one correctly," said Aadi running towards it.

*Wusssshhhhhhhh...*went off the first one suddenly with effusing fire.

Aadi jumped and fell on his back again. "Haha. It tricked us," he said with a burst of awkward, croaking laughter.

Subbu and Jambu took over after that. Subbu fired up some rockets, and Jambu did the remaining moon shots. Aadi was trying to figure out the art of lighting-up bhoo-chakras. Adhvika and Sumati were making designs in the air with sparklers, and just like that, through the dazzling lights of the fireworks, Adhvika noticed a familiar face sitting under the tree at a distance across the street.

"Hey Sumati look," said Adhvika pointing towards the person.

"Bolu!" gasped Sumati hurtling towards the tree.

Bolu was gazing at all the fireworks when he noticed Sumati and Adhvika coming toward him. He looked at them appalled, leaning backward as if to defend himself, wondering what trouble he might have caused, quickly trying to think through in his mind, if any.

"Whew! Mr. Bolu, there you are," said Sumati panting. "Where have you been?"

Bolu looked petrified.

"No, nothing to worry about. We are here to apologize," she said.

He looked, now, perplexed.

"You helped us without even asking," continued Sumati. "Yet I was impolite and didn't even thank you properly."

Bolu wobbled his head side-to-side as if he was following.

"It was not intentional. I was preoccupied with so many things…"

"I am sorry," Adhvika cut in, "I rubbed off all my negative influence on her. It's not her fault."

"No—no, Adhvika. It's not fair that you take the entire blame. I volunteered for it. You didn't say a word about those lights. It's me. I am sorry," said Sumati.

Bolu continued wobbling with astonished glee.

"The thing is Bolu, we all have these energies. They kind of have a ripple effect, if you know what I mean. They bounce off each other, impacting us while simultaneously pulling us into it. All the time, while we remain oblivious to it," explained Adhvika.

"And today, we had some not-so-good moments. We inadvertently became part of such bad energy due to circumstances," said Sumati.

Bolu continued wobbling his head side-to-side with his mouth open, but he now had a dazed and much more perplexed look.

"Nevertheless, Bolu, thank you so much for your help today," Sumati said appeasingly.

He broke into a slightly nervous smile, still wobbling.

"Happy Diwali!" said Adhvika.

Bolu was completely smiling now while the wobble continued.

There was a

pause. And then Sumati said, "Would you be able to join us for dinner? It would be great if you could."

Adhvika nodded. Bolu continued to wobble his head.

"So yes? Say something," asked Sumati as if to be sure.

"Diwali—Di—Dinner—yes...yes...my pleasure..." said Bolu with a glint in his eyes and a confused face as he began to walk back slowly.

"Where are you going? See you in a few?"

"Yes. I'll be there shortly...shortly," he picked up speed as he galloped and shouted, "*Finally Diwali has come...Adbhuta!*"

"Ok, you know where we live," muttered Sumati as they slowly walked back home.

Chapter 8:

Utsava Bhojana - The Feast

It was well into the night now, and the sounds and lights of fireworks began to taper off, at least in the neighborhood where Pulis lived. Sumati and Adhvika informed others about Bolu joining them for dinner. As Adhvika heated the food, the house got engulfed in the appetizing and hunger-galvanizing smells. Sumati and Jambu helped set the table with the dishes as they were warmed and ready to go. They also set up a few diyas and tea candles on the dinner table, while Aadi got the utensils and water. Subbu started chomping anything and everything he could get his hands on. They heard a tiny knock on the door. Bolu was standing there coyly in a ravishing red kurta and a box in his hand.

"Ah! You must be Bolu, come in," said Subbu, tapping both his shoulders. "What's in that box?"

"Basundi," he replied timidly.

"Basundi! Oh my! Where from?" asked Subbu with invigorated excitement.

"Vinayak Rao Sweet Shop, across the community park."

"Oh, should be what—just ten mins, at most, from here?" said Subbu in a confirming voice while digging into the box with a spoon. He took a big serving out of the box and put it in his mouth. "Hmm...so creamy," he said, closing his eyes and then thundered. "*Aadi!* You never told me about Vinayak Rao."

"Vinayak Rao, who?"

"The sweets store."

"There are dozens of them. How many would I be able to tell you about?"

"But you never mentioned basundi to me," snapped Subbu.

"Bolu!" interjected Sumati in excitement as she came out of the kitchen carrying the last set of warm dishes, "Thank you for coming. Make yourself at home."

"Come in, have a seat," welcomed Jambu.

"Bolu got this basundi box. So good, so good..." said Subbu mesmerizingly.

Slowly everyone got settled near the dinner table.

"Bolu, so nice of you that you got us some treats," said Adhvika pleasantly.

"Hehe...thank you," replied Bolu shyly.

"You didn't have to do it," said Aadi.

"Well, my mom always said, never show up empty-handed to anyone's home. Especially on festivals and other occasions. And more so specifically, on Diwali," said Bolu smiling shyly.

"Ah, Traditions! Love them," said Subbu with his eyes on the feast set on the table.

"This house. Decorations. Especially that diya setup and the rangoli around it, so-oo good, adbhuta!" he said, showing the first signs of comfort since Adhvika and Sumati met him initially.

"Thank you!" replied Adhvika happily.

"The lights you helped set up outside are also very adbhuta, just like that basundi," said Subbu with his eyes still on all the food as if he was making calculations on how to consume every food item out there without getting full.

"Hehe," Bolu chuckled, and his face lit up as he said, "This reminds me of home."

"Glad you say that," said Aadi with a smile, as all others nodded.

"Adhvika ji, Sumati ji, and all of you, thank you for making me a part of your Diwali dinner. And this food, so many dishes. Abbo-abbo-abbo...Adbhuta," said Bolu exhilaratingly and shrunk back immediately into a diffident demeanor as he felt the gaze of everyone looking at him.

"It's our pleasure Bolu! Let's start dinner," said Adhvika to remove the attention from Bolu so that he could be himself.

"You are our guest. Please go first," said Sumati, handing the plate to Bolu.

While everyone started piling up their plate with food, Jambu's plate looked sparse. Just one roti so far. "Sumptuous!" he said, putting in a couple of spoons of cucumber carrot salad. He dabbed some raita into his plate to go with it. Served himself a spoon of curry and said, "That should be adequate," as he sat down in the chair, placed his plate on the table and rubbed his hands to relish.

"Jambu, are you not feeling well?" asked Aadi.

"Do you have health issues or dietary restrictions?" wondered Sumati making sure to clarify.

"Why do you ask?" said Jambu innocently.

"Pfff..." Subbu stifled a snigger looking at Jambu's plate.

"Oh, you mean my plate. Ha! No worries, I'll eat some more if I feel like it. It's just that I follow a simple regimen. Less is more...What's all the fuss about anyway. This is a feast to me," he smiled and waved his hand dismissively as if they were being unreasonable.

"*But it's Diwali Today!*" said Adhvika in anguish as she served food to Bolu, making sure he was not being hesitant.

"Ahem! Let me explain...Diwali or not—" Jambu started.

"Jambu," interjected Adhvika angrily with a serious look and said, "Huh, all these apprehensions, done with your restrictions. Today is Diwali. It's time to be generous and jolly..."

It came out like a song, almost, but a very stern one. Everyone stopped eating and looked at her.

She took a deep breath, smiled, and sang...

No more apprehensions, keep away restrictions...
Today is Diwali, be generous and jolly.
Haha-haha-hahaaaa—Haha-haha-hahaaaa—Heyhey-heyhey-
heyyyy...

"Haha-haha, Heyhey-heyhey! What a song," mumbled Subbu with amusement and he saw the dishes and continued as if he got the cue...

Ah! The pulihora! With its magnificent aura.
Relish this payasam, so delicious and awesome.
Haha-haha-hahaaaa—Haha-haha-hahaaaa—Heyhey-heyhey-
heyyyy...
Subbu and Adhvika sang the last line together.

Aadi took a bite and said, "Ssssss..."
Eat this mirchi bajji, so fiery and feisty,
Should it make you sweaty, fear not! There is lassi.
All three of them sang.
Haha-haha-hahaaaa—Haha-haha-hahaaaa—Heyhey-heyhey-
heyyyy...

"Jambu! Adhvika put so much work into these..." said Sumati sounding despair, as she ate a spoonful and crooned,
Dal bati churma, so yummy Rama Rama!
Pass me the korma and spare me the drama.
Even Bolu sang along,
Haha-haha-hahaaaa—Haha-haha-hahaaaa—Heyhey-heyhey-
heyyyy...

Bolu looked at all the food in happiness and murmured, "So much food..." And then he sang...
Laddoos and pedas. Samosas, pakodas.
I am lucky as lolly...delighted as Diwali!

Everyone but Jambu while thumping the table in chorus,
Haha-haha-hahaaaa—Haha-haha-hahaaaa—Heyhey-heyhey-heyyyy...

Now, everyone looked at Jambu seriously, as if it was his turn and he better come up with something good. "Alright! Enough!" said Jambu, looking at everyone equally serious, "Love the gobi paneer..." slowly changing into a mischievous smirk,
Love the gobi paneer. It comes with Diwali cheer.
As you all go crazy, I'll devour kaju katlis.
He took a handful of them. "Yay..." shouted everyone and sang,
Haha-haha-hahaaaa—Haha-haha-hahaaaa—Heyhey-heyhey-heyyyy...

Adhvika being the ever-caring host,
There is also mishti bonde and the creamy basundi,
Kindly eat fully and say happy Diwali.
Everyone loudly in chorus,
Haha-haha-hahaaaa—Haha-haha-hahaaaa—Heyhey-heyhey-heyyyy...

Somewhere in another part of the Dvipa, Hima, while enjoying food with her family,
Hot hot vadas...spicy wicey chutneys,
Dig into these malpuas and enjoy the festivities.
Haha-haha-hahaaaa—Haha-haha-hahaaaa—Heyhey-heyhey-heyyyy...

In Bose colony, "*Pappely rasam...yum...kastar—ahum—ahem,*" coughed Minnu.

"Careful, dear. Drink some water. Don't swallow everything. You have to bite and eat slowly," said Shyam Lal concernedly.

Minnu squeaked, "Yumm…"

That peppery poppery rasam, this fruity nutty custard.

Shyam Lal sang,

(As) I see you bright and shiny, my heart goes Diwali.

They sang along…

Haha-haha-hahaaaa—Haha-haha-hahaaaa—Heyhey-heyhey-heyyyy…

All the singing about food invigorated Subbu. There is no stopping him now. He became creative and recited passionately throwing each hand in the air alternatively,

Colorful rangolis, mehendi kachoris, fluffy chola-pooris.
Light thousand diyas, have aloo bondas, chomp dozen momos.
Jug-aty mug-aty sambar, that you'll ask baar baar,
crispy crunchy appadam, (fire)cracker goes Doom! Daam!…

In the end, had both his hands in the air as he said it.

"It's a tad bit…too much," said Sumati, twitching one of her eyes.

"We didn't even make all those foods…" said Adhvika sheepishly.

"Who cares…We have enough for our entire street to feast…It's just a song, just sing along…" roared Aadi. "Today is Diwali, be generous, crazy and jolly…"

As they all bellowed in laughter.

Haha-Haha-hahaaaa—Haha-haha-hahaaaa—Heyhey-heyhey-heyyyy…

As they enjoyed the festive dinner. Praises were heaped upon

Adhvika and Sumati for their efforts in making the wonderful dishes and thanks were sent to Aadi and Adhvika for being wonderful hosts. Adhvika promptly returned the gratitude to everyone for helping with all the preparations. Subbu prattled at length on the sour and sweet conglomeration and conflict of what he thought was a wonderful lassi. Bolu shared his story, career aspirations, and his not-so-fortunate results so far. Jambu chimed in with his words of encouragement and advice, while others joined in with other suggestions that left Bolu elated and gave him a lot to think about. They touched upon Shyam Lal and Minnu. Connecting Shyam Lal to Hima Harin was one of the ideas, while probably relocating his store to a better location might just do the trick was the other opinion. Supporting Minnu's education was something they all agreed upon. The discussion wandered around daily affairs and after a while, Bolu announced its time for him to leave and thanked them again for their hospitality. Aadi and Subbu saw him off to the gate. As they came back to continue the talk.

"Next year, I want to start decorations soon after Dussehra and keep the cheer going till Diwali," declared Adhvika.

"And I want to keep the Deepavali decorations till Karthika Poornima," announced Sumati.

"Ah! That sounds good. Whatever and however you do it, make me a part of it," said Jambu.

"That's a given. You don't have to mention it specifically," replied Aadi, sounding obvious.

"As long as there are ladoos and payasam I don't mind celebrating festivals the entire year," mumbled Subbu dazedly. He was half asleep with all the food.

"Talking of that, what mithai and desserts do you like the most?" asked Sumati.

They chatted at length about their favorite foods, which woke

Subbu up.

"Aadi, I know you mentioned you don't like cashew nuts, but you should try—" said Subbu.

"Wait—" cut in Aadi, "When did I say that?"

"Earlier Today, when we arrived at your place and discussed pulihora..."

"I didn't say that. I was responding to—" Aadi tried to explain.

"But Aadi, I did hear you bring up something about cashew nuts," said Adhvika.

"Yes, me too," Sumati chimed in.

"Did anyone listen to what he actually asked and what I—"

"Ah! Don't be a kid now. Doesn't matter if you don't like cashew nuts, but what I meant to say is—"

"*Alright!*" said Jambu, "that tells me it's time to call it a night. What a wonderfully festive day it was...Happy Deepavali again!" said Jambu. "Happy Diwali!" said the rest of them as they ended the night happily.

Jambu's Letter

Dear Children,

I write to you from the little town of *Balluka Nagari*, near the foothills of majestic Himagiri ranges in the northern part of Vajra Dvipa. It's my favorite time of the year; the tri-festive time or 44 days of autumn festivities! It starts with the Season of Dasara (Navratri/Vijayadasami), continues with Diwali and ends with Karthika Poornima. For some, it even goes on further for another 15 days. It goes without saying, Diwali, among these, is the brightest and most exuberant.

The stories, the auspicious reasons, and the beliefs behind this festival are multitude. To my good knowledge, there is no way I could list down all of them. Nevertheless, let me try. Celebrations of joy and lights that occurred when the ever-beloved Mother Sita and Lord Rama returned to Ayodhya after 14 years of exile, and after destroying the demon king Ravana and his army of evil is the most prominent and considered by many to be the primary reason behind the festival. Likewise, in some traditions, the destruction of evil by Lord Krishna and Satyabhama, or Mother Kali is believed to be the reason. Importantly, this festival marks the birth of Lord Dhanavantari and Lakshmi Devi, signifying health and wealth. Nirvana (liberation) of Lord Mahavira is said to have happened on this night, and the celebration of lights symbolizes his life. Also, the revered Guru Hargobind, who, along with himself, led to the release of 52 kings from the imprisonment of Mughals, resulted in similar celebrations with processions and lights. For a few, the mighty emperor Ashoka treading the path of Buddha's message of peace and enlightenment is the reason for celebrating this festival. Not to forget Kedara Gowri Vrata: Worshipping Lord Shiva and

Mother Parvati is another important ritual followed in a few cultures for this season.

Ah! By now, you might have realized what I meant when I said I couldn't do justice in covering all of them. But if you notice, all these events, stories and traditions converge with a unifying message of celebrations of good, light, positivity and warding-off evil, darkness and negativity.

If we extend our curiosity further in the exploration of the roots of this festival, it also carries a deep seasonal significance. In the Northern Hemisphere, we are at the end of Ashwayuja Maasa (Or the middle of Karthika Maasa, depending on the lunar tradition followed). Sharad Ritu, aka Autumn bells, are peaking and are in their full glory, and in some regions, during certain years, they might as well be ending, signifying an impending onset of Hemantha Ritu (pre-winter). During such times of the year (October 15 to November 15), as days begin to get visibly shorter-especially in temperate climate zones, nature begins on a slow rescind, and as we prepare ourselves to make a transition into the upcoming winter months as if for us to serve as a remembrance, to keep the light in us always ignited resisting any negativity due to the impending slowdown, the darkest night of the season aka Amavasya (new moon night) is celebrated as "Deepavali'' aka Diwali, signifying knowledge, light, and positivity!

In the Southern Hemisphere, though, it's Vasantha Ritu, aka Spring. What other better occasion than this, to let the divine festive light guide everyone to remain humble as the celebrations magnify due to the happiness this season naturally brings.

Now delving a little bit into the traditions, they too are many and diverse. Cleaning and decorating houses, buying new clothes, making elaborate feasts, gift exchanges, family get-togethers, prayers, parties, charities, and honoring animals that we interact with daily are some of the traditions followed in various regions. One belief is that our ancestors who descend to the planet to check on our well-being during the autumn season head back to the heavens during Diwali time; hence we light up and make sounds (crackers) to guide them on the darkest night. Interesting, isn't it?

The festival itself spans 5 days. Day 1: Dhanavantri Trayodashi or Dhanteras. Day 2: Naraka Chaturdashi or Kalichaudas. Also known as Chhoti Diwali, aka little Diwali. Day 3: The actual festival day, Deepavali/Diwali. Day 4: Balipratipada/Govardhan Puja. Day 5: Bhai Dooj. Each day has its own cultural and spiritual significance; what they mean is beyond this letter's scope. That would be for you to research. But I will tell you this, depending on your region and local culture, the festival could be celebrated for one day, five days, or anywhere between. Doesn't matter how many days or how we celebrate and whatever our reasons and beliefs might be, the most common and unifying traditions of setting up diyas and lights, bonding with family and friends, making good memories to cherish for the future, and the spirit of happiness and positivity that unifies us is what I love the most about this festival.

With cheers of a bountiful harvest, the hustle and bustle of the markets, as families and friends get together to exchange gifts and wishes and the streets fill up with the smells of festive feasts, the sounds of celebrations, and as the darkest of nights lights up with the brightest of lights, it signals the arrival of this beautiful festival, *Deepavali*. Let me take the opportunity to wish everyone happiness, health, and prosperity on this occasion.

Happy Diwali!
From,
Your beloved,
Jambu

Glossary

Aakasa Deepa: Translated as light in the sky. In this book, Aakasa Deepa implies a lantern made of cloth or paper with a wooden framework used as a decoration hung outside the house. The common name for it is Kandeel. *{from Sanskrit Aakasa: space or sky; Deepa: light}*.

Aagamana: Arrival.

Aarambha: Beginning.

Abbo-abbo-abbo: Expression of amazement.

Adbhuta: Wonder, marvelous.

Amavasya: New moon night.

Anjali Mudra: A mudra or pose formed by bringing both palms together and generally holding them closer to the chest in reverence or respect. *{Namaste: Is Anjali Mudra generally combined with a verbal gesture}*. A mudra is a sacred or symbolic gesture.

Astagiri: Eight mountain range; *{from Sanskrit Giri: mountain, hill; Asta: eight}*.

Basundi: Sweetened-condensed milk garnished with nuts.

Bhakti: Faith, devotion, reverence, worship.

Bhinnatva Nagari: Town of Diversity. *{from Sanskrit Bhinnatva: Diversity; Nagari: Town, Settlement}*.

Bhinnatva Nagari References:

Below words loosely mean greetings or good wishes on the occasion of Diwali/Deepavali/Deepotsav in various Indian Subcontinent languages *{from Sanskrit - Shubha: Good, auspicious}*

- **Deepavali Subhakankshalu** - Telugu.
- **Deepavali Valthukkal** - Tamil.
- **Deepotsavam Ashamsakal** - Malayalam.

- **Diwali ki bahut bahut badhai ho** - Hindi.
- **Diwali ki dher sari shubhkamnaayein** - Hindi.
- **Diwali Ni Shubhkamna** - Gujarati/Parsi cultures.
- **Diwali Shubhechha** - Marathi.
- **Shubh Deepavali** - Hindi.
- **Shubh Laabh** - Wishing goodness and prosperity - Hindi.
- **Shubo Dipaboli** - Bengali.
- **Shubo Kali Pujo** - Happy worship of mother Kali (day before Diwali) - Bengali.
- **Tihar ko Shubakamana** - Tihar wishes {*Tihar is how Nepalese and few Indian regions of Sikkim and North Bengal refer to Deepavali as*}.

Gujarati:
- **Diwali aavi, sathe ghani khushiyon laavi:** Diwali brought lots of happiness.

Hindi:
- **Mu meeta karo**: Phrase used for celebrations, happy occasions and good news, loosely translated as *sweeten the mouth*.

Kannada:
- **E jagadalli Annadaana**: Food Donation service here.

Punjabi:
- **Langar**: Community kitchen serving food.

Tamil:
- **Deepam Vilakethu:** Light up the Deepam.

Telugu:
- **Dayacheyandi:** Please come in.
- **Gavvalu:** Shell-shaped sweet treats made with flour, milk and sugar.
- **Murukulu/Janthikalu:** A deep-fried noodle-like snack made from chickpea or rice-based dough infused with various spices.

- **Palakova:** Thickened milk sweetened with sugar and cardamom, cut into small pieces.
- **Panduga:** Festival.
- **Poothareku:** A sweet that is made of sugar/jaggery, nuts, and raisins and stuffed into a paperlike sheet made of rice powder and then weaved into multiple layers. {*Pootha: coating, Reku: sheet*}.

Bhoo-chakra: A rotating fireball-like firework that goes off on the ground.

Brahma-Muhurta: The pre-dawn morning hours before sunrise is considered auspicious. {*Muhurta of Brahma*}.

Crufflasia A cookie-like holiday dessert from the lands of Sufaria.

Dakshina: South.

Dasara/Dussehra/Dashain: Also known as **Vijayadasami,** a major festival that occurs at the end of Navratri i.e 10th day. At times Navratri+Vijayadasami, the entire ten-day season, is referred to as Dasara/Dussehra season in a generic sense. {*from Sanskrit Vijaya: Victory; Dasami: Tenth day*}.

Deepa/Deepam: Light ; Clay lamp.

Deepavali (popularly called Diwali): Translated into a Row of lights. It's also known as Deepotsav (festival of lights), Tihar, Swanti. Spelling variations include Deepawali, Dewali, Divali, Dipavali. {*from Sanskrit Deepa: Light(s); Avali: Row of, Line of; Utsav: Festival, Celebration*}.

Diya: A lamp made of clay (unless specified) that uses oil/ghee/wax and a wick to emit light flame.

Dvipa(s)/Dweepa(s)/Dweepam: Continent(s), Island(s). In this book, Dvipa refers to a continent while Dweepam is for an island. {*Sakaii Dweepam: Island of Sakaii; Vajra Dvipa: Continent of Vajra*}.

Flowerpot: Effusing sparkling fountain kind of a firework.

Food Song References:

- **Aloo bondas:** Ball-shaped fluffy fritterers made of chickpea flour stuffed with mashed potatoes, curry leaves, onions and various spices.

- **Appadam/Appalam/Papadam/Papad:** Deep fried or dry heated item made of black gram dough (at times, other lentils, millets or rice doughs could also be used). Used as a starter or accompaniment.

- **Baar baar:** Again and again.

- **Chola puri:** A sort of bread and chole curry combination. {*Chole/ Chola: Chick-peas curry; Puri (Poori): Deep fried bread typically made from unleavened whole wheat flour*}.

- **Dal bati churma:** A dish made of three distinct items served with dollops of ghee. {*Dal: Lentil soup (typically made of a combination of different lentils for this dish); Bati: Wheat balls; Churma: Crushed wheat or bajra mixed with sugar and ghee and made into a powder*}.

- **Gobi paneer:** Used as a reference to cauliflower paneer curry.

- **"Haha-Haha-hahaaaa—Haha-Haha-hahaaaa—heyhey-heyhey-heyyyy":** Phrase inspired from 'Vivaha Bhojanambu' song-Mayabazar Movie.

- **Kachori:** Deep fried snack stuffed with lentils and spices mixture.

- **Korma:** A cream based (from yogurt or coconut milk or cream) curry made of vegetables or meat.

- **Lassi:** Yogurt-based drink, thick buttermilk. Variations of lassi include using salt and spices, or sweetened using sugar and fruit pulps.

- **Lucky as lolly:** Just used for rhyming purpose.

- **Malpua:** Sugar syrup-coated pancakes made with a batter of flour (wheat, semolina or all-purpose), yogurt, spices, milk or khoa, cardamom and topped with nuts. Various fruit pulps or coconut also could be added to the batter.

- **Mirchi Bajji:** A fried fritter made of green chili.

Mishti bonde: A deep-fried sweet made from a batter of chickpea or rice flour poured into the oil through a holed vessel producing small spherical-like structures. Which then are soaked in sugar syrup.

- **Mithai(s):** Sweets, confectionaries.

- **Momos:** Bite-sized dumplings (steamed or deep fried) stuffed with vegetables or meat.

- **Payasam, Payasa:** Dessert made with rice/millets, milk, ghee, sugar/jaggery, nuts, raisins, cardamom.

- **Pulihora,Puliyogare:** Tamarind rice (sometimes implies lemon rice) tempered with spices, lentils, jaggery.

- **Rasam:** A soup like dish made of tomatoes, tamarind, spices and herbs. Typically eaten with rice.

- **Raita:** A side dish made of yogurt, spices and vegetables like onions, cucumbers, cilantro.

- **Roti:** A round flat bread typically made of wheat.

- **Sambar:** Lentil, vegetables and tamarind stew infused with various herbs and spices.

- **Samosa:** Triangle or tetrahedron-shaped deep fried crispy snack made of all-purpose flour stuffed with potatoes, spices, herbs and, at times, onions, peas, and other vegetables.

- **Vadas:** Savory fried snack made from lentil batter. They are typically made into a doughnut, spheroid, or a flattened circle shape.

Garam: Hot.

Ghanta: Sacred bell. The bell is rung to welcome the divine. The sound from it is considered auspicious.

Ghee: Clarified Butter.

Hing: A pungent smelling spice. Asafoetida is the scientific name.

Holi: Spring festival of Colors.

Ji: Mark of respect.

Kaju Katli: Cashews paste mixed with sugar solution and cut into slices (typically diamond shaped) decorated with edible silver foil. At times Ghee, saffron and other nuts are also added. {*Kaju: Cashew; Katli: Slice*}.

Kanti/Kaanti: Light, beauty, brightness.

Karthika Poornima/Pournami: A major festival that occurs exactly 15 days after Diwali, on a full moon night; {*Karthika: Month of Karthik, Poornima/Pournami: Full moon night.*}

Kolam/Muggu: Like Rangoli. While Rangoli is more of a free art form, kolam uses a fixed grid pattern with repetitive designs. Though increasingly, such differences are going away. A simpler form of kolam/muggu is drawn at the entrance of households every morning.

Kumbhams: Slang word to imply lots of or a pot full of.

Laddoo/Laddu: A spherical-looking sweet typically made using ghee, sugar, lentils/nuts/other ingredients.

Ladis: String bombs that go off in a quick sequence.

Mantra(s): Depending on the context used it could have a variety of meanings. Some of them include,

- Words/Sounds that have sacred meaning.
- Words with magical power.
- Words that could cause extreme energies (Constructive/Destructive).
- Guideline/Pathway to something that's being referred to.

In this book its used in the below ways,

- During Puja time: A group of words that have sacred meaning, meant to carry a lot of positive energy.
- During normal conversations between characters: As a rule that could guide our life.

Maasa/Maasam: Months. 2 different forms of lunar calendars are followed in Vajra Dvipa to track months (referenced from the Indian system). The first one goes from full moon to full moon. Similarly, the second one goes from the new moon till the next new moon. As per the first system, Diwali occurs in the middle of Karthika maasa. As per the second calendar system Diwali happens at the end of Ashwin/Ashwayuja maasa, and the day after Diwali, karthika maasa begins.

Mehendi (Mehndi/Mehandi/Henna): Ancient body art farm, typically used plant-based paste on hands and legs. A very common tradition for festivals and important events like marriages.

Muhurta: A division of time. In colloquial language, it is commonly used to denote an auspicious hour to perform ritual.

Nadhi(s): River(s).

Naivedya: Food prepared for the occasion that is first offered to gods or food exclusively prepared to be offered to gods.

Navratri: An auspicious festival celebrated for Nine nights, an event that occurs 2 times a year but is typically referred to as the one that comes in Sharad ritu, i.e., autumn season. {*Nav: Nine; Ratri: Night(s)*}.

Om Sri Maha Lakshmiyei Namah: A Mantra meaning salutations to great Lakshmi Devi.

Pakodas: A deep-fried fritter made of gram flour, vegetables, and spices.

Paneer: A cottage cheese made with curdled milk solids separated from whey.

Pasuman: Animal-like looking person {*Pasu: Animal (Typically domesticated)*}.

Pedas: Similar preparation as palakova but also further enriched with nuts and saffron and cut into small spherical shapes.

Prakasa: Splendor, glow, glory.

Prasada: A part of Naivedya consumed by devotees after the puja.

Puja: A worship ritual, spiritually celebrate an event.

Rajbhog-Rasgulla: Rajbhog and Rasgulla refer to two different variations of a sweet made with a base of clamped curdled milk (paneer balls) and sugar syrup. In this story context, it is used as a single sweet combination.

Rangoli: Is an art form and a ritual in which various designs and geometric patterns are put on floors, at the entrances to homes and at times on table tops. Various colors and flower petals are used to further accentuate the designs. There are similar art forms with different names and variations throughout the Indian subcontinent Kolam, Muggu, Alpana etc. Diwali, Sankranti/Pongal, Onam are some festivals during which rangoli or other variations are common. {*Derived from Sanskrit "Rangavalli"*}.

Rasmalai: A sweet made of clamped curdled milk, i.e., paneer balls that are put in saffron, cardamom-infused thickened/sweetened milk. {Ras: Juice, Malai: Cream}.

Ritu: Seasons. Below are referred to in Jambu's letter.

- **Sharad:** Autumn (September - Mid-November).
- **Hemanta:** Pre-winter (Late November - December).
- **Sisira:** Winter (Late December - February).

Samudra(s): Gathering of waters, that receives all waters. Used to refer to Oceans and Seas.

Sarve Janah Sukhino Bhavantu: A Sanskrit verse that means May all live in happiness and peace.

Sashtanga pranama: Prostrating on the floor with reverence. Though Sashtanga pranama is used generically, there are differences like Ashtanga Pranama, meaning full prostrate with eight body parts touching the ground vs Sashtanga pranama with six body parts touching the ground vs. panchanga (five) vs dandavat(two).

Sufaria: Another continent on the planet of pasumans.

Suklam Baradharam Vishnum Sasivarnam Chaturbhujam: Stotra from Vishnu Sahasranamam (a Sanskrit hymn containing 1000 names of Vishnu). {*Stotra: A hymn of praise*}.

Sutli bomb: High decibel hydro bomb.

Tri-festive Season: Denotes the entire season, comprising three important festivals. Dasara/Dussehra (including Navratri), Diwali/Deepavali and Karthika Poornima/Pournami. Spanning 44 days. (59 days if extended till the end of Karthika Month). It generally spans Autumn (Sharad) and pre-winter season (Hemanta).

Utsava Bhojana: Festive feast. {*From Sanskrit Utsava: Festive; Bhojana: Feast*}.

Uttara: North.

Vaibhavapuri: A city in Vajra Dwipa. {*From Sanskrit Vaibhava: Magnificient; Puri: City*}.

Vajra Dvipa: Continent of Vajra. {*From Sanskrit Vajra: Indestructible, Diamond*}.

Varahas: A form of currency in the world of Pasumans; Reference used from Vijayanagara Empire coinage.

Vishnu Chakra: A rotating fireball kind of a firework that goes off in air, held by a firm metal wire away from the body.

Siva K. C. Penamakuru was born and raised in the Telugu lands of Southern India. He moved to the U.S. in 2005 for his master's education and now lives there with his family. If not working at his day job as a software professional, Siva spends most of his time with his family reading books, cooking and exploring new cuisines/recipes, and traveling. Festivals and holidays became a crucial part of Siva's cultural moorings growing up, which he cherishes to date. *Let There Be Light - A Diwali Story* is one such attempt to share his love for the festival of Deepavali with the larger world.

Sara Kuba is an illustrator with an affinity for all things cute, bright, and whimsical. She graduated from Ringling College of Art and Design with a B.F.A. in Illustration in 2018, and has been pursuing her love of illustrating children's books ever since. She aims to educate, edify, and encourage children with her fantastical and heartfelt illustrations. When not drawing, Sara enjoys playing video games, crocheting, and shopping at thrift stores.

Printed in Great Britain
by Amazon

31722792R00067